"Don't look at me like that!"

Alejandro growled the command in husky chastisement.

"You don't understand!" The air seemed charged with emotional intensity.

"You think not?"

Elise gained nothing from his tone of voice. "Alejandro—"

"It is no less difficult for you to be faced with a husband you fail to recognize than it is for me to have the woman who is my wife look at me as if I were a stranger!"

HELEN BIANCHIN was born in New Zealand and traveled to Australia before marrying her Italian-born husband. After three years they moved, returned to New Zealand with their daughter, had two sons, then resettled in Australia. Encouraged by friends to recount anecdotes of her years as a tobacco share-farmer's wife living in an Italian community, Helen began setting words on paper, and her first novel was published in 1975. An animal lover, she says her terrier and Persian cat regard her study as theirs as much as hers.

Books by Helen Bianchin

HARLEQUIN PRESENTS
1423—THE STEFANOS MARRIAGE
1527—NO GENTLE SEDUCTION
1561—STORMFIRE
1601—RELUCTANT CAPTIVE
1704—PASSION'S MISTRESS
1741—DANGEROUS ALLIANCE

Don't miss any of our special offers. Write to us at the following address for information on our newest releases.

Harlequin Reader Service
U.S.: 3010 Walden Ave., P.O. Box 1325, Buffalo, NY 14269
Canadian: P.O. Box 609, Fort Erie, Ont. L2A 5X3

Helen Bianchin

Forgotten Husband

Harlequin Books

TORONTO • NEW YORK • LONDON
AMSTERDAM • PARIS • SYDNEY • HAMBURG
STOCKHOLM • ATHENS • TOKYO • MILAN
MADRID • WARSAW • BUDAPEST • AUCKLAND

ISBN 0-373-11809-0

FORGOTTEN HUSBAND

First North American Publication 1996.

CHAPTER ONE

SHE didn't want to open her eyes. Not yet. For when she did, *he* would be there.

The man they said was her husband, seated in a chair to one side of the bed where she'd been told he had maintained an almost constant vigil for days after her admission.

For the past week he had confined his visits to three each day—early morning, mid-afternoon, and evening.

The nurses had commented on it when they thought she was asleep...and relayed it in informative, faintly envious tones when she was awake. Together with the added news, her initial admission had caused a furore. It appeared that within an hour of being transported unconscious by ambulance from the accident scene to a nearby public hospital all hell had broken loose, and she had been transferred post-haste to this exclusive and very expensive private establishment with its coterie of consultant specialists.

'Elise.'

The voice was a deep, faintly inflected drawl, and its timbre succeeded in tripping her pulse into an accelerated beat.

Damn. Now she would have no recourse but to acknowledge his presence. Her lashes trembled fractionally, then fluttered slowly upwards.

His physical impact was such that it took considerable effort not to close her eyes again in an attempt to shut out the sight of him.

A tall man, whose impressive breadth of shoulder and impressive frame, even in relaxed repose, was intimidating. Broad, sculptured facial features were harshly chiselled, all angles and planes as if etched from stone, and his eyes were so dark that they appeared black—almost as black as his well-groomed hair.

Beneath the cool mantle of his sophisticated façade he bore the look of a hunter, as untamed as a savage jungle beast and just as dangerous.

Alejandro Santanas. Even his name was unusual, and the relayed information she had been given was merely statistical, rather than enlightening.

He was in his late thirties and he headed a financial empire whose very name was regarded with due reverence in the business sector.

A very wealthy man, one of the nurses had revealed, whose entrepreneurial skill ranked him high among the upper echelon of the country's rich and famous.

Elise didn't find it surprising, for there was an inherent degree of power, a ruthlessness lurking beneath the surface, which she found vaguely frightening.

The knowledge that she was his wife had initially shocked and dismayed her, for each individual nerve-end had screamed out in denial that she could be bound to him in any way.

Dammit, she didn't *feel* married, she agonised silently.

Nor did she feel pregnant. Yet there was an ultrasound picture as proof that the seven-week foetus in her womb had suffered no harm.

His child.

Never in a million years could she imagine that she'd fallen in love with him ... or he with her.

Yet there were wedding-photos taken six months previously to prove their legal alliance, and not once during the many times she'd examined them had she been able to detect anything other than pleasure in her captured smile.

Depicted on celluloid, the top of her head barely reached his shoulder, lending her slender frame a visual fragility. Honey-blonde hair worn in a shoulder-length bob framed a finely boned face, and her eyes were wide-spaced, her mouth a generous curve.

Yet when she looked in the mirror she saw a stranger, with pale symmetrical features and topaz-flecked green eyes.

Losing one's memory, even temporarily, was akin to standing in front of a door to which there was no key, she thought in silent anguish. The answers lay out of reach on the other side.

Amnesia after such an accident was not uncommon, and in her case the condition was temporary. With no indication of *when* her memory would return, she'd been advised that while some patients regained total recall within days, others experienced intermittent flashes over a period of several weeks before everything finally fell into place.

'Good morning, *querida*. You slept well?'

His voice was deep and vaguely husky, and Elise watched with detached fascination as his wide mouth curved into a warm smile.

Why ask, she felt like querying, when you've undoubtedly elicited that information from the attendant sister before entering my suite?

'Yes.' The monosyllabic response held restraint, and she silently examined her need of it. 'Thank you,' she added politely, all too aware of the studied darkness evident in his eyes.

Shouldn't there be some level of recognition deep within her psyche, *anything* that would allow her to *know* him? Even if her mind failed to acknowledge him in any intimate capacity, surely an instinctive sixth sense would force some kind of awareness?

Dammit, she cursed silently. It wasn't *enough* to have to believe that Alejandro Santanas had swept her off her feet in a whirlwind courtship. The fact that they had married a month later in Sydney left too many details unexplained.

A natural curiosity about her background had been partially satisfied by examining a thick album containing family snapshots, although there was a sense of disappointment when not one of them managed to rouse a spark of recognition.

In the past week she had leafed countless times through the many pages filled with glossy prints depicting her from infancy through childhood, highlighting scholastic and sporting achievements, accenting her chosen career as a paediatric nurse. There were photos of her parents, the mother she had lost at an early age, and several of her father, whose affection for his only child was achingly apparent . . . all the more poignant, given that he had recently died. Holiday snaps taken with friends she was unable to identify. The suburban family home Alejandro informed her she had shared with her father until her marriage. Altogether they encapsulated the past twenty-five years of her life.

'Your hand?' Alejandro queried lightly. 'It is less painful this morning?'

'A little,' she responded stiffly, refusing to relay that her ribs and her shoulder still ached, and that her heavily bandaged right hand, in which surgeons had inserted titanium pins to align several fractured bones, felt stiff in its supportive splint. It could have been worse, the medics had assured her, considering that the other vehicle had run through a 'Stop' sign and ploughed head-on into the passenger side of her car.

'Is there anything you need?'

Elise closed her eyes, then slowly opened them again. 'You send me flowers every day.' Unbidden, her gaze skimmed to the huge bunched masses of exotic blooms—roses, varying in hue from pale cream to the deepest red, their long stems and velvet petals attesting expensive hothouse origin, exquisite arrangements assembled with delicate artistry and dispensed, according to one of the nurses, from one of Sydney's most exclusive floral boutiques. 'And fruit.' A bowl containing a varied selection stood within easy reach. 'I have so many magazines...' She made a visible effort to inject a little warmth into her voice.' What more could I possibly want?'

'To come home, perhaps?' Alejandro queried with teasing indolence, his dark eyes intently watchful as she attempted to veil her startled expression.

Dear God, *no*. It was a silent scream dredged up from some hidden recess deep within her soul. The hospital, this particular suite, represented a sanctuary she was reluctant to leave. Yet she couldn't stay indefinitely.

She swallowed, aware of the slight lump that had risen in her throat, and her fingers began pleating the sheet's hem in abstracted agitation. 'I am to be released?' She looked at him carefully, attempting to read something more from his expression, yet his features were relaxed and his mouth curved to form a warm smile.

'The neurologist and obstetrician have each assured me there is no reason why it should not be this afternoon.'

So *soon*. Why couldn't it be tomorrow, or the day after? At least then she would have time to get used to the idea.

Now, the thought of re-entering the home she purportedly shared with him filled her with inexplicable dread.

It was difficult to pinpoint her reluctance. Was it because there had been no one, other than Alejandro Santanas, to visit her?

She could accept that she had no immediate family, but what of her friends?

Was he such a possessive man that he wanted her entirely to himself, to the exclusion of all others?

She searched his features and saw the assurance evident, the strength of character, and perceived that he was a force to be reckoned with, a man no adversary would choose to have as an enemy.

And as a lover? A shiver of apprehension slithered down the length of her spine. One couldn't live with such a man as he and be unaware of his sexuality... or remain unawakened to her own. Without doubt he would have introduced her to every intimacy, every sensual pleasure, and taught her precisely how to respond in kind.

'Don't look at me like that,' Alejandro growled in husky chastisement.

Elise closed her eyes in silent chagrin, then opened them again, her gaze wide with a mixture of puzzlement and confusion. 'You don't understand.'

The air seemed charged with emotional intensity, and she seemed to be having trouble regulating her breathing.

'You think not?'

She gained nothing from his tone of voice. 'Alejandro——'

'It is no more difficult for you to be faced with a husband you fail to recognise than it is for me to have a woman who is my wife look at me as if I were a stranger.'

In seeming slow motion she watched as he clasped her uninjured hand and lifted it to his lips, and a gasp emerged from her throat as he gently turned it palm upwards and buried his mouth in the soft hollow.

Acute sensation arrowed with unerring accuracy to the core of her femininity, flooding it with a heavy languorous warmth, and she was held mesmerised by the depth of emotion evident in his eyes.

'Do you have any conception what it does to me to see your eyes dilate with apprehension every time I touch you? To be aware you would prefer my lips brush your cheek, rather than possess your mouth?'

The room, its contents, faded to the periphery of her vision, and she could only look at him, unable to utter so much as a word, the moment seemingly freeze-framed in time.

The knock at the door proved an anticlimax, and she hurriedly tugged her hand free as the kitchen orderly carried in a breakfast-tray.

'Morning,' the woman greeted cheerfully as she placed the tray on the bed-trolley, then slid it into position before turning towards the man seated close to the bed. 'Can I bring you some coffee, Mr. Santanas?'

Alejandro's smile curved the edges of his mouth, deepening the vertical creases that slashed each cheek. 'Thank you, no.'

Elise watched as he unfolded his lengthy frame from the chair. Leaning forward, he covered her mouth lightly with his own, and her lips trembled beneath the brief contact.

'Your discharge is scheduled for two o'clock. *Hasta luego, querida.*'

For one crazy second she felt strangely bereft, almost wanting more than that fleeting touch, and something flickered in the depths of his eyes before it was successfully hidden, then he straightened and moved towards the door.

Elise watched his departing figure with perplexity. The warmth of his lips against her own, the restrained degree of passion that lay just beneath the surface had stirred her senses, almost as if some inner being were intent on forcing recognition.

'There you are, Mrs Santanas,' the kind-faced kitchen orderly declared as she undid a mini packet of cereal and added it to the bowl of fresh fruit. 'Which spread would you prefer on your toast?'

Hospital routine ensured that there was little time in which to brood, Elise accorded wryly, for within ten minutes of the breakfast tray being removed a nurse arrived to assist her in the shower, followed by the doctor's round, physiotherapy, morning tea, the daily visit from the hairdresser—arranged, she had been informed, by her husband.

It was a thoughtful gesture, although she couldn't help attempting to analyse his motivation. And that proved detrimental, for it only brought her relationship with Alejandro Santanas to the fore, and incurred a renewed bout of soul-searching.

It seemed ludicrous to doubt Alejandro's depth of caring when there was every evidence of his devotion in this room: the cards carefully placed together in the drawer of her bedside pedestal, each bearing 'Love', written in black ink, and signed 'Alejandro' in a powerful slashing hand.

More importantly—did *she* love him? Certainly she'd married him, but was *love* her motivation?

Dear heaven, she wasn't the sort of woman who had deliberately contrived to trap a wealthy man by using feminine wiles . . . was she?

Elise closed her eyes in silent anguish, then slowly opened them again.

'Time, *patience*,' the neurologist had stressed solemnly. Yet such an answer was as frustrating as it was ambiguous.

Lunch was a delectable bowl of beef consommé, followed by thin slices of roast beef with accompanying vegetables, and segments of fresh fruit for dessert.

Apprehension began to knot in the region of her stomach, only to intensify a short while later as a nurse entered the suite.

'Your husband will be here to collect you in half an hour,' she informed Elise with a bright smile. 'I'll help you dress, then pack your things.'

I don't want to go, an inner voice screamed in silent rejection. Several jumbled thoughts raced through her head. Perhaps she could dream up a mild complication—the onset of a headache, her hand—*anything* that would delay her departure.

Yet even as she contemplated such an action she dismissed it as futile and, pushing the bedcovers aside, she slid to her feet, watching with detached fascination as the nurse moved to extract clothes from a nearby closet.

Sage-green trousers in uncrushable silk, a cream silk blouse, wispy briefs and bra in matching cream silk and lace, low-heeled shoes. Each item looked incredibly expensive, and undoubtedly was, given the evident reverence with which they were handled.

Elise stood still as her nightgown was removed, an exquisite garment in peach satin-finished silk and lace, which made up a set with its matching négligé.

Obediently she stepped into the briefs and helped draw them up, then the trousers.

'I'll use the outermost clip,' the nurse declared as she carefully slipped the bra into place before adding the blouse. 'If it's not comfortable, we'll take it off. Would you like some help with your make-up?'

There was a case holding everything imaginable, but all she'd chosen to use over the past week was moisturiser and a pale lipstick. Perfume? Her fingers hovered near the curved glass bottle of Dior, then retreated. She hadn't bothered to use it in hospital, so why begin now?

Elise watched with idle fascination as the nurse extracted a valise and began filling it with all her belongings.

'Please,' Elise intervened as the girl caught up a variety of glossy magazines. 'Keep them.'

'Are you sure?'

'Yes. And the flowers,' she added. 'Divide them among the day and night staff. And the fruit, the chocolates.'

The nurse's features mirrored her gratitude. 'Thanks. They'll be appreciated.'

Elise's mouth curved into a soft smile. 'You've all looked after me with great care.'

They had, despite it being their job to do so. Yet there had been a marked degree of dedication to this particular patient.

Because of the man whose very presence demanded nothing less? Or was it the faint air of mystery, the haunting vulnerability of the attractive girl who had occupied this suite?

'Sister will be here in a moment to formally sign you out of the hospital system.'

Elise murmured something suitable in response, and gazed sightlessly after the nurse's departing form.

Why did she feel so uncertain and so damnably insecure? A natural reaction, an inner voice assured her, in tones remarkably like those of the consultant neurologist.

The door swung open and she turned towards the ward sister, accepted the relevant appointment cards, and listened to the professional advice which concluded with, 'Don't attempt anything too strenuous too soon.'

'I will personally see that she doesn't,' a faintly accented masculine voice assured her from the doorway, and Elise turned slowly to face her husband.

The business suit he had worn that morning was absent, replaced by dark trousers and a polo shirt unbuttoned at the neck. The casual knit fabric emphasised his breadth of shoulder, the long sinewed sweep to his taut waist, and revealed powerfully muscled forearms liberally sprinkled with dark hair.

His smile was warm, and Elise idly watched the nurse's reaction with detached fascination, aware of the faint appreciative gleam evident beneath the professional façade.

Did all women respond to Alejandro Santanas in this way? Elise wondered silently. Such thoughts were hardly conducive to her peace of mind, and she stood very still as he moved towards her and brushed his lips against her temple.

'I have the car waiting outside.'

Her indecision must have been apparent, for his gaze narrowed slightly as it took in her pale features and the degree of uncertainty evident in her deep green eyes.

'You have no need to feel apprehensive,' he assured quietly.

Are you kidding? she wanted to scream. I'm being taken to a home I can't remember with a man I feel I hardly know.

With a sense of desperation she sought to elicit some sort of recollection—*anything* that would provide her with a measure of reassurance.

Yet there was nothing, and she cursed herself afresh for attempting to force a situation over which she had no control.

'If you'd care to follow me,' the ward sister suggested, 'I'll accompany you to the main entrance.'

His frame seemed to overpower hers as they traversed the carpeted corridor, and her stomach executed a series of painful somersaults as she caught sight of a large, expensive-looking vehicle parked immediately adjacent to the main doors.

Indisputably his, it looked as powerful as the man who owned it, and she slid carefully into the passenger seat, unconsciously holding her breath as he leaned forward to attend to her seatbelt.

His hand brushed against her breast, and her pulse leapt, then set up an agitated beat as he carefully fastened the clip in place, leaving her feeling helplessly trapped.

Oh, God. She had to control her over-active imagination, she counselled silently as he closed the door and crossed round to slide in behind the wheel.

The car eased forward and she experienced the insane desire to tell him to stop and let her out, which was crazy, for where could she go?

Minutes later the large vehicle emerged into the steady stream of traffic, and with a sense of resignation she focused her attention on the scene beyond the windscreen.

Houses constructed of bricks and mortar; neat garden borders bearing a variety of brightly coloured flowers; carefully tended lawns; trees lining the streets, their wide spreading branches providing shade from the sun's shimmering rays; numerous electronically controlled intersections; shops.

It all appeared so normal, so everyday. Yet none of it looked familiar.

Some of her tension must have made itself felt, for Alejandro turned slightly and cast her a discerning glance.

'You are uncomfortable?'

Her eyes widened slightly as she met his dark gaze, and she uttered a polite negation before he returned his attention to the road.

The car's air-conditioning reduced the force of the midsummer heat, and Elise breathed a silent sigh of relief as he activated the stereo system, glad of the music's soothing qualities, for it precluded the necessity to converse.

With seeming fascination she observed the quality and style of the houses lining the wide arterial road begin to change, from small, dark, weathered brick structures sited on small blocks of land to those of larger and more stately design.

Old mingled with new, their elegant façades revealing a visual attestation of wealth.

The celluloid print Alejandro had shown her of their home in suburban Point Piper revealed a large double-storeyed mansion overlooking the harbour. How long before they reached it?

'A few more minutes,' Alejandro told her quietly, almost as if he knew the passage of her thoughts.

CHAPTER TWO

THE large vehicle slowed to a halt before a set of ornate steel gates which opened at the touch of an electronic modem, then closed just as quietly behind them as Alejandro eased the car along a wide sweeping driveway.

The double-storeyed house was an architectural masterpiece in cream cement-rendered brick and floor-to-ceiling tinted glass, its tiled roof a dazzling silver-white, and set well back from the road in beautiful sculptured grounds, whose neat garden borders and profusion of flowers and shrubs were visual proof of a gardener's loving care.

The car drew to a halt at the main entrance where an impressive set of heavy panelled doors was offset by a pair of large ornamental urns, and once inside Elise was unable to prevent a faint gasp in awe of the spacious foyer.

The central focus was a tiered marble fountain, complete with gently cascading water, above which an ornate crystal chandelier hung suspended from the high glass-domed ceiling which lent spaciousness and light. A wide double staircase curved up to an oval balcony from which opposing hallways led to two separate wings.

Exotically designed panels of stained glass in the huge atrium shot brilliant prisms of multi-coloured light on to the pale walls, magnifying their pattern in an ever-changing sweep controlled by the direction of the sun's rays.

'It's beautiful.' The words slid unbidden from her lips, and she moved forward to pause at the marble fountain. 'Were you responsible for the design?'

His eyes were dark, almost still, then he smiled. 'To some degree—yes. I consulted with numerous experts in order to achieve this result.'

She put out a hand and trailed her fingers through the water, soothed by its soft flow against her skin, then she turned slightly towards him.

'You must entertain a great deal.'

His slow smile held warmth. 'There are occasions when it is more relaxing to invite business associates to one's home,' he responded indolently.

'With their wives?' Where did that come from? A natural assumption, she assured herself silently. Successful men had wives or mistresses. Some presumably had both.

Did Alejandro possess a mistress?

He took the few steps necessary to her side and placed a hand beneath her elbow. 'Let us go into the lounge. Ana will have made tea, and prepared a few delicacies to tempt your appetite.'

At the silent question mirrored in her expression, he added quietly, 'Ana takes care of the house and does the cooking. Her husband José looks after the grounds, the cars, and acts as general handyman.'

His nearness bothered her more than she was willing to admit, and she walked at his side as he ushered her into a beautifully furnished room which commanded a splendid panoramic view of the inner harbour.

Expensive works of art were spaced at intervals on the silk-covered walls, and provided an elegant backdrop for the magnificent Chinese rugs that covered the marble floor. Predominantly pale blue, employing a delicate mix of cream and the palest pink in their patterned design, the large rugs were a perfect foil for the cream-upholstered sofas and chairs, the rosewood cabinets and profusion of glass-topped occasional tables.

No sooner had Elise selected a single chair and settled comfortably into its cushioned depths than a pleasantly plump woman of middle years entered the room, wheeling a trolley on which reposed two steaming pots, milk, sugar, cream, and various plates containing a selection of small cakes, pastries, and delicate sandwiches.

'It is so good to have you home again,' Ana greeted as she poured tea, added milk and sugar, then placed the cup and saucer within easy reach on a glass-topped table beside Elise's chair.

'Thank you.' It seemed strange to be faced with a woman she must have dealt with on a daily basis in the six months of her marriage.

'I will make dinner for seven o'clock. Is there anything special you would like?' The smile broadened with pleasure. 'You have often complimented Ana on her chicken soup.'

Elise injected warmth into her voice. 'Chicken soup will be fine.'

'And afterwards? An omelette, with mushrooms, some cheese, a little tomato, ham?'

'That sounds delicious,' she qualified, watching idly as Ana poured coffee into a demitasse and handed it to Alejandro before leaving the room.

The tea tasted like liquid ambrosia, and Elise took a small sandwich, savouring the delicate smoked salmon and cream-cheese filling, accepted another, then declined anything further.

'More tea?'

'Please,' she acceded gratefully, watching his lengthy frame unfold from the chair. His movements were measured and concise, his hands sure and steady as he refilled her cup and replaced it within easy reach.

'Have you lived here for very long?' The need to converse seemed paramount, and her fingers shook slightly as she lifted a hand and smoothed back an imaginary lock of hair behind one ear.

His eyes flared slightly at the nervous gesture, and she made a conscious effort to dampen the edge of panic threatening to assume unmanageable proportions.

'A few years. I had the original house removed, then began from scratch.'

She felt as if she were on a conversational roller-coaster that she couldn't stop. 'During the past week I've looked at photograph albums which mean very little, and you've provided essential information. Tell me more about how we met, and why.'

His smile assumed musing indulgence. 'The need to fill in some of the gaps?'

'There are so *many*.'

'And you are becoming impatient.'

'Frustrated,' Elise corrected. 'I seem to have a hundred questions.'

'All of which you want me to answer at once?'

Her eyes took on a haunted quality. 'I *need* to know.'

'You walked into my office demanding a minimum five minutes of my time.'

'*Why?*'

'Your father had borrowed extensively from my merchant bank, and you refused to accept my decision not to extend the loan or the term.'

She digested the information slowly. 'You own a merchant bank?'

'I have many investments,' he revealed solemnly.

'Was I successful in overturning your decision?'

He seemed to take his time in answering. 'You could say we eventually reached an understanding.'

'You asked me out.' This much she knew, because he had told her.

'You opposed me as no other woman had, questioning my business acumen and condemning me for my lack of compassion.' Warmth gleamed in the depths of his dark eyes. 'Your fierce loyalty impressed me, and I was sufficiently intrigued to insist we share dinner. Within twenty-four hours I had persuaded you to marry me.'

'And arranged for the wedding to take place a month later.' Dear God. Such omnipotence was devastating. She found it vaguely shocking that she had given her consent. 'Am I supposed to believe you're an honourable man, or go with reality?'

One eyebrow slanted in mocking cynicism. 'Which reality would you prefer, *querida*?'

'You have the advantage,' she managed, with a degree of sadness. 'While I possess none.'

'Finish your tea,' he commanded quietly. 'Then I will take you upstairs to rest.'

She wanted to say that she wasn't in the least tired, but the thought of being free from his disturbing presence for an hour or two was attractive, and she replaced her cup on its saucer.

'I have a house overlooking the ocean at Palm Beach. It's an ideal location for you to relax and recuperate.'

'You mean for both of us to stay there?' Not *alone*, surely? she agonised, aware that he had caught the fleeting emotions apparent on her expressive features.

He lifted a hand and brushed warm fingers across her cheek. 'Of course. Your welfare is very important to me.'

For some inexplicable reason she felt the faint stirring of apprehension feather insidiously down her spine.

Why? she queried silently as they moved towards the magnificent staircase. Yet with every step she took, her sense of anxiety increased.

The entire floor was covered in thick-piled powder-blue carpet, providing a cool tranquillity that was pleasing.

Elise caught glimpses of rooms employing muted shades of pale green and peach, delicate pinks and greens, the softest shades of blue and cream, all so beautifully co-ordinated that she began to suspect he had enlisted the services of an interior decorator.

The master suite held a king-sized bed and two finely crafted rosewood chests of drawers, with matching cabinets and bedside pedestals. The drapes and bedcover were of a bold design in cream, pale lilac and blue.

She watched as he crossed to the bed to turn back the cover, then with deft movements he retrieved several pillows from a cabinet and assembled them into a comfortable nest against the bedhead.

'There's an intercom device on the pedestal,' Alejandro informed her as she slid off her shoes, then sank back against the pillows.

The breath caught in her throat as he lowered his head and brushed his lips against her own in a provocative caress before straightening and moving back a pace.

'I'll be in the study for an hour or two. If you need anything, just activate the intercom. Rest well, *querida*,' he bade gently, then he turned and left the room.

There was a collection of magazines conveniently placed within easy reach, and Elise idly browsed through two before discarding them, her eyes heavy with a weariness she could no longer fight.

Her sleep was dreamless, and when she woke it was to see Alejandro standing a short distance from the bed, his eyes dark and faintly brooding as they examined her pale features.

'I'll have Ana bring you a tray.' He reached out a hand and tucked a stray tendril of hair back behind her ear. 'Come,' he commanded, sweeping the sheet aside. 'I'll help you undress.'

No, a silent voice screamed from deep within. 'I should be able to manage,' she voiced in strangled tones.

'I doubt it,' Alejandro returned, his eyes darkening measurably at her evident reluctance. 'Think of me as a nurse,' he drawled, taking in her clear-eyed resolve with a narrowed gaze as she got to her feet.

No nurse of the male species could possibly look as he did, nor create such havoc with her senses.

Calm deliberation was evident in his actions as his fingers undid first one button, then another.

'The thought of a man you can't remember removing your clothes,' Alejandro pursued in a silky voice, 'a man who as your husband has lain with you every night in this bed, tasted every inch of you, and placed the seed of his child in your womb... *frightens* you?'

'Unnerves me,' Elise corrected shakily, almost hesitant to voice the words that had tortured her since she had been made aware of her pregnancy. 'Had we *planned* to have this child?'

His eyes took on a gleaming warmth as he leant down and brushed his lips to the edge of her mouth. 'The choice and timing of conception was your decision.' His fingers freed the third button, then moved to the fourth. 'Rest assured, I could not be more delighted.'

The last button slid undone, and she stood helplessly still as he slipped the silk blouse free from her left arm, removed the sling supporting her injured right hand, then carefully drew the blouse free.

When he reached for the clip fastening on her bra she was unable to prevent an intake of breath or govern the erratic beat of her heart, and she would have given anything not to be dependent on his help.

'Close your eyes, if you must,' he advised with amused indulgence. 'Unfortunately I cannot do the same, for fear I might cause you unnecessary pain.'

He was amused, damn him! Resentment flared, lending her eyes a brilliant sparkle as she sprang into barely restrained speech.

'You think I enjoy being dependent on you?' Stupid tears welled up and threatened to spill.

'Your reticence is somewhat misplaced,' he chastised as he freed the clip, then eased the straps off each shoulder, and his eyes narrowed as she lifted an arm to cover her breasts.

A protesting gasp escaped from her lips as he caught hold of her left wrist and carefully pulled it away.

She closed her eyes, aware of her bruised shoulder. The colour had changed from dark red to purple. Now it was a deep bluish-green.

'*Por Dios*.' The soft curse slipped into the stillness of the room, and his eyes darkened in silent anger as he saw that the bruising extended the length of her ribs on the right side.

The silence stretched between them, and began to play havoc with her nerves.

'It could have been worse,' she offered, and saw his expression harden into a frightening mask.

'Yes,' Alejandro agreed with brutal cynicism. 'That young fool behind the wheel could have been responsible for your death.'

His eyes travelled to the soft swell of her breasts, and she remained helplessly still as he trailed gentle fingers over their rounded contours, shaping first one, then the other, before brushing a thumb-pad across one tender peak.

Elise gasped out loud as pure sensation shot through her body, arrowing down to focus at the junction between her thighs, unleashing a multitude of feelings she wasn't sure how to handle.

A distressed whimper escaped her lips. 'Please,' she begged, her eyes clouding with anguish as he traced a path to the soft hollows at the base of her throat, then lingered over the rapidly beating pulse for a few heart-stopping seconds before trailing up to rest at the edge of her mouth.

'You look so incredibly fragile, it robs me of breath,' he ventured slowly, his dark eyes so deeply piercing it seemed as if he possessed licence to see into the depths of her soul.

Elise swallowed convulsively, and let her lashes flutter down to form a protective veil, only to have them fly open as the tip of his finger slowly outlined the generous lower curve of her mouth, teasing the soft fullness until it parted involuntarily, allowing him to continue the sensual probe.

A slight tremor shook her slim frame, and she was powerless to move as he slowly lowered his head to close his mouth over hers in a provocative, sensual tasting that was so incredibly gentle it almost made her weep.

Some deep intrinsic need prevented her from moving away, and she bore the light sweep of his tongue as it explored the sweet recesses of her mouth, creating an acute sense of loss as he slowly withdrew. For several long, timeless seconds her eyes were held mesmerised by his, then his lips curved into a slow, warm smile as he reached for her nightgown and eased the straps over her injured hand, then her head, before pooling the silk at her waist while he removed her trousers and briefs.

'Do you need help in the bathroom?'

'No,' she refused, infinitely relieved that this was an area there was no need for him to invade.

'I'll be back with a tray in ten minutes.'

Oh, dear God, she breathed silently as the door closed behind him. What was happening to her? How could she react so damnably with someone her conscious mind failed to recognise?

She had made no effort to move away from the touch of his mouth, merely stood mesmerised as he had initiated a sensual foray that had played havoc with her vulnerable emotions.

'There are two dinner-plates,' Elise declared with a slight frown as Alejandro re-entered the room and set the covered bed-tray into position across her lap.

One eyebrow lifted in quizzical query as he subjected her to a long, considering look from beneath dark-fringed lashes. 'You imagined I would leave you to eat alone?'

She had hoped he might. He emitted a sensual vibrancy that was intense—*dangerous*. To envisage him as a lover was sufficient to set alarm bells jangling inside her brain, awakening feelings deep within that raised questions she had no desire to answer.

'Eat, Elise,' Alejandro commanded. 'Before the food becomes cold.'

Obediently she picked up the spoon and started with the soup, then when it was finished she used a fork to dissect the omelette.

It was impossible not to be aware of him as he sat a few feet distant in a comfortable chair. His movements were economical, and her eyes were drawn to the strength of his jaw, his mouth.

Remembering how that mouth had felt against her own brought a flood of soft colour to her cheeks, and she couldn't help but wonder what it would like to be kissed by him . . . really kissed, not the controlled brushing of his lips against hers that had been little more than an affectionate salutation.

He looked the sort of man who would *consume* a woman—with a deep, drugging passion that gave no quarter, demanding an abandonment so complete that there could be no room for reticence.

She did not know the measure of her own personality, or the strength of her emotions. Yet even in her wildest imagination she couldn't imagine acting like a wanton in his arms.

He had said he had tasted every inch of her. He couldn't mean . . .

'You have finished?'

His query startled her, and she met his unfathomable gaze with widened eyes. 'Yes. Thank you. I'll be fine now,' she added quickly in dismissal, and saw his eyes narrow slightly as he removed the tray.

He regarded her steadily, his expression revealing, and there was latent steel beneath the velvet tone of his voice. 'The bed is sufficiently large to accommodate both of us.'

The thought of sharing the bed with him made her stomach knot with unenviable nerves. 'I'd prefer a room of my own.'

'No.'

It was a categorical refusal. One that made her uncommonly resentful. 'I think——'

'Don't *think*,' Alejandro advised with dangerous softness, and her eyes acquired an angry sparkle.

'How can I *not*?' she declared, with a degree of asperity. 'I have no knowledge of you in any sexual sense. I know I'm not ready to resume intimacy. Dammit,' she flung heatedly, 'I can't even remember if we're——'

'Sexually compatible?' he drawled in silky query. 'I assure you we are, *mi mujer*. Passionately, primitively so.'

The retort she wanted to fling at him died in her throat as he began unbuttoning his shirt. No matter how hard she tried she couldn't prevent her gaze from focusing on him, watching beneath lowered lashes as deft fingers competently dealt with remaining shirt-buttons before moving to free the belt at his waist. Seconds later the shirt was tossed over a nearby chair, closely followed by his trousers.

It was impossible not to be aware of his impressively muscled frame: broad shoulders, chest tapering down to a trim waist, slim hips and long, powerful thighs.

Something deep inside her stirred, then slowly unfurled at the sight of his chest, liberally covered with whorls of dark hair which arrowed down over a taut waist to disappear beneath black silk briefs.

'Are you going to join me in the shower?'

He had to be joking!

Elise's eyes widened measurably, then grew dark as her gaze shifted to a point somewhere beyond his right shoulder, and she was powerless to stop the faint flood of colour covering her cheeks as her imagination ran riot.

'I can cope on my own,' she managed in strangled tones, hating him as he calmly scooped her to her feet.

She wanted to hit him, or at the very least hurl abuse at his merciless head. Sparks of topaz accentuated the green of her eyes, and her chin tilted in open defiance. 'I hate having you play nursemaid,' she said with a degree of anguish as he carefully undressed her.

'I refuse to stand by and have you inflict further damage on your shoulder out of a foolish need for modesty.'

The tone of his voice should have warned her, but she was too angry to take any notice. 'And I dislike the thought of a husband who practises voyeurism.'

He stiffened, his large frame an awesome sight as he held himself severely in check. Anger emanated from every pore, and his eyes were so dark that they resembled polished onyx. 'Perhaps you should give thanks to the good *Dios*,' he intoned in a hard voice. 'If it were not for your injuries, I would teach you a lesson you would not easily forget.'

As he had in the past? Dear God, was he an abusive man? she agonised in shocked silence. Her features paled at the thought, and she heard him utter a string of viciously soft incomprehensible words.

'Go and have your shower, Elise,' he commanded with dangerous silkiness.

She needed no second bidding, and her mouth set in mutinous lines as he followed her into the bathroom and switched on the water, tested its temperature, then stood aside as she stepped into the large stall.

Despite the rising cloud of steam she was aware of his presence a few feet distant on the other side of the glass screen, and she gritted her teeth against rising anger, feeling no remorse for taking longer than necessary before closing the taps.

He was waiting as she slid open the glass door, and her eyes waged a silent battle with his as he stepped forward and removed the waterproof covering from her bandaged hand, then collected a towel and began blotting the dampness from her body.

'I'm quite capable of completing the task,' Elise said tightly, and almost swayed beneath his long, intent gaze.

Did he have any idea of how vulnerable she felt? How damnable it was to have to stand naked before him and suffer his ministrations?

'Of course,' he drawled with hateful amusement as he discarded his briefs and stepped into the shower.

There was an enviable selection of toiletries to choose from atop the long marble vanity unit, and after making use of a few Elise collected a large towel and was about to secure it sarong-wise around her body when the water stopped.

Seconds later the door slid open and Alejandro emerged from the stall.

Elise hastily averted her eyes from the electrifying image of his superbly muscled frame, with its generous mat of curling chest-hair arrowing down in a fine line past his navel to join the hair couching his manhood.

There was something incredibly erotic about glistening water droplets caught in male body-hair, the fluid grace of strongly honed muscle-fibre moving beneath satiny, lightly bronzed skin.

The degree of restrained power in repose was an intensely disturbing entity, and her fingers shook as she caught up a brush and stroked it vigorously through the length of her hair, increasingly aware of his every action as he towelled himself dry.

As he reached for a black silk robe she stepped quickly into the bedroom, almost succeeding in donning her nightgown before firm fingers eased the straps over her injured hand, and she stood helplessly still as the silk hem whispered down past her hips.

Impotent resentment darkened her eyes, and Alejandro cast her a long, thoughtful look which she found increasingly difficult to hold as the seconds ticked slowly by.

He lifted a hand and slid firm fingers beneath the hair at her nape, then in seeming slow motion his mouth claimed hers with an element of possession she instinctively knew would harden should she attempt to pull free of him, and she swallowed convulsively as pleasure overtook warmth, touching each nerve-end as it coursed through her body.

She felt strangely afraid—not of him, but of herself, and the wild sweetness that swirled within, encouraging a response she was hesitant to give.

His tongue sought out every secret recess, every ridge, before lightly stroking her own tongue in an erotic dance that reached deep into her feminine core, unleashing emotions almost beyond her control.

She was slowly melting, awash in a sea of delicious sensation, totally unaware of voicing a faint murmur of regret as he slowly lifted his mouth from her own.

'Into bed, *querida*,' Alejandro bade firmly.

Within minutes of her head touching the pillow her eyes became heavy, and it was easier to give in to somnolence than fight it.

Alejandro stood for a long time in contemplative silence, his gaze dark and brooding as he surveyed her finely boned features, the sweep of blonde hair, the delicate texture of her skin, the long, thick eyelashes and the sweet curve of her generous mouth, softly swollen from his kiss.

A muscle tightened at the edge of his jaw, then he reached forward and switched off the lamp on the nearby pedestal before crossing to the other side of the bed to ease his long body carefully between the sheets.

Seconds later he snapped off his own lamp, and focused his attention on the shadowed ceiling.

CHAPTER THREE

THE heat of the summer sun was reduced to a comfortable level by the car's air-conditioning, and Elise leaned back against the leather-cushioned seat as Alejandro slotted a disc into the stereo system.

'This is a beautiful car,' she commented with genuine appreciation as it swept noiselessly along the arterial road heading north.

'A Bentley,' he enlightened her, shooting her an amused glance.

'It looks expensive.' The words slipped out unbidden, and his eyes narrowed slightly.

'A luxury that affords me pleasure,' he responded in a soft drawl that sent a shivery sensation feathering down the length of her spine.

As I do? Is that all I am to you . . . a possession?

Permitting her thoughts to travel such a path was both fruitless and detrimental; it served no purpose.

'You have been remarkably docile all morning,' he relayed musingly. 'I could almost believe you are treading eggshells.'

'I woke early, and couldn't get back to sleep,' she proffered, for it was no less than the truth.

He slanted her a frowning glance. 'You should have woken me.'

'Why?' She attempted a smile, and almost made it. 'So we could both have lain awake?' *How could* she tell him that she had experienced a gamut of emotions as she had watched him sleep? His strongly etched features had been barely visible in the darkness and then, as the dawn sky began to lighten the room, she had been held spellbound by the stark beauty of his countenance in repose. The harshness was gone, his jaw and mouth relaxed, and his lashes curled slightly, their length and shape dark and lustrous. Fascinated, she had wanted to reach out and place a finger against the edge of his mouth, to trace a slow pattern over the firm curve and watch him stir into wakefulness, to open his eyes and witness their warmth as he caught sight of her. Instead, she had feigned sleep the instant he looked like rousing, and only stilled the pretence when she had felt him rise from the bed.

Afterwards she had managed to dress herself, and on descending the stairs a startled Ana had immediately led her out on to the terrace to join Alejandro for breakfast.

'The car I was driving . . . was it badly damaged?'

Alejandro slowed the Bentley to a halt at a set of traffic-lights, then turned to slant her a probing glance.

'You are more important to me than any vehicle.'

Was she? 'You didn't answer the question.'

'It will be several weeks before you gain medical clearance to get behind the wheel of a car. And, when you do, it won't be a fashionable sports model. Meantime, José can drive you wherever you need to go.'

She looked at him in stunned silence for several seconds before venturing in protest, 'You can't be serious.'

'Unequivocally.'

Elise added another quality to his character. Inflexibility. 'Are you usually this...overbearing?'

'Protective,' he corrected. 'You could have lost the child. Worse, I could have lost *you*.'

The lights changed, and his attention returned to the road ahead. As the Bentley gathered speed Elise evinced an interest in the passing scenery.

There were many coves and inlets, picturesque beaches, crisp sand, softly waving tree-branches stirring beneath a gentle breeze, and an expanse of glorious blue sea that stretched out to the horizon to merge with the sky.

'How long before we reach Palm Beach?'

'About forty minutes, depending on traffic.'

It was just after midday when Alejandro swung the car into a driveway leading to an imposing double-storeyed house overlooking the ocean.

It was the antithesis of what she had imagined a beach-house to be, and once inside there was a sense of unreality as he led her through several rooms on the lower floor. Beautifully furnished, it was almost as magnificent as the Point Piper mansion. There was even a swimming-pool adjacent to the terrace— almost a decadent addition, given the accessibility of the ocean a few short steps distant.

The upper floor held four bedrooms with *en suite* facilities, and as she followed Alejandro into the largest suite Elise couldn't help but wonder how frequently he made use of the house.

'Do you come here often?' she queried, watching as he deposited their bags.

'Whenever I can manage a few days away.'

Crossing to the large picture window, she moved the curtain fractionally to admire the view. Sun-dappled water, a few cruisers anchored offshore, young children, supervised by their mothers, playing happily in the sand. 'It looks so peaceful.'

She sensed rather than heard him move to stand behind her, and sensation stirred deep within, lending an awareness that made her feel acutely vulnerable. His body warmth seemed to enfold her, and all the fine hairs on her skin rose up in instinctive self-defence.

'The precise reason why I bought the place,' he told her.

'An escape from the wheeling and dealing of high-powered executive city living?'

Was that why she felt such an empathy with the house? Because it represented a refuge? From what...*whom*? The man who owned it?

She gave a sudden start as his hands rested lightly at her waist, and there was no way she could disguise the frisson that shook her slim frame as his lips settled against the curve of her neck.

'Alejandro...' Her voice faltered, then regained a measure of strength. 'I'd like to go downstairs,' she said, on a note of desperation. He was too *close*, much too close. It bothered her, and she couldn't reason why. 'Lunch,' she elaborated, and felt immeasurably relieved when he disengaged his clasp and moved fractionally away.

'Then we shall eat. The fridge and pantry are well-stocked.'

Elise turned slowly to face him. 'You're going to play cook?'

He lifted a hand and trailed gentle fingers across her cheek, letting them slide down the edge of her jaw to tilt her chin.

She gazed at him in mesmerised silence, taking in the hard planes and angles of his broad facial structure, the vertical crease that slashed each cheek, the powerful sweep of his jaw, the wide mouth.

'You find the prospect of being alone with me so daunting?'

He was teasing her, and suddenly it seemed so unfair that he had the advantage while she had none.

Indecision and a fleeting sense of mild panic coursed through her veins, visible in the dilation of her eyes as she gazed at him.

His eyes darkened and became almost black. 'Little fool,' he growled gently. 'You look at me as if you are struggling with fear. What manner of man do you imagine I am?'

'I don't know,' she was forced to own, aware that it was nothing less than the truth. Of all the details she had been made aware of, few had given a hint of his character.

'Come,' Alejandro directed, releasing her chin. 'We'll go down to the kitchen and find something to eat.' He bent down and brushed his lips against her own with the lightness of a butterfly's wing. 'In a few days you will become accustomed to having me around.'

Somehow she doubted it. Yet she accepted that she had no choice but to try.

In the kitchen he retrieved cooked chicken from the refrigerator, divided it into portions, and placed several on a platter to heat in the microwave. Then he prepared a wholesome salad with a deftness Elise found surprising. Within a matter of minutes there was food on the table.

'Please,' she protested as Alejandro began filling her plate. 'That's too much.'

'Eat what you can,' he bade easily, employing his cutlery to divide her food into bite-sized segments which she could manage with a fork.

There was a studied intimacy in his actions, a familiarity she tried desperately to recognise, yet she could recall nothing that gave a hint of the many meals they must have shared together.

'Why the slight frown?'

'Did we socialise much?' she ventured, quickly qualifying the question. 'Both your homes are large.'

'It is all too easy to gather a coterie of acquaintances who are active on the social circuit,' he answered. 'Unless you become selective, it is possible to spend three nights out of every seven at one dinner party or another.' His eyes assumed a teasing warmth. 'Since our marriage, I have chosen to entertain only when necessary, and much prefer dining *à deux* with my beautiful wife.'

Yet a man of his calibre would be in demand, his friends many and varied. Her position as his social hostess seemed a foregone conclusion.

'Why not eat?' he suggested quietly. 'The chicken will become cold.'

It looked appetising and, aware of her own hunger, she picked up her fork and speared some chicken, then salad, repeating the action until she felt replete.

'Some fruit?'

She selected an apple, its white flesh crisp and tangy, and when she'd consumed it she sat back in her chair.

'Iced water?' Alejandro queried, and she shook her head in silent negation. 'Why not go upstairs and rest?' he prompted gently. 'I'll take care of the dishes, then join you.'

'Your solicitude is overwhelming,' Elise said quickly, alarmed at his intention. 'But hardly necessary, when you must have calls to make, people you should contact.'

His gaze was remarkably steady, and a faint smile lifted the edge of his mouth. 'And you prefer to be alone,' he drawled.

'Yes,' Elise answered honestly, and glimpsed a degree of humour lurking in the depths of his eyes. Because you scare the hell out of me, she added silently. Every defence mechanism I possess screams out a warning of one kind or another, yet I'm unable to fathom *why*.

It was a relief to reach the sanctuary of the bedroom, and she selected a magazine, then sank back against the pillows.

She dozed, and when she woke there was a note, scripted in black ink, signed by her inimitable husband, informing her that he was in the study.

It took only minutes to freshen up and go downstairs, and Alejandro glanced up from a sheaf of papers he was examining as she entered the study, a slow, teasing smile curving the edges of his mouth.

'You look rested,' he commented musingly, and her heart tripped its beat, accelerated for a few seconds, then settled into a steady pattern.

His smile was lazy, extending to the depths of his eyes, and he rose to his feet with a lithe indolence, crossing round the desk in a few easy strides.

His head lowered to capture her lips with openmouthed gentleness, and she felt like crying *Don't* out loud as she stood helpless against the trembling sensation slowly consuming her body. The desire to sway towards him shocked her, and she experienced a mixture of emotions as his lips left hers.

Relief, dismay—*regret*? She didn't want to analyse her emotions, and she gave a shaky smile as he caught hold of her hand.

Alejandro exchanged long trousers and shoes for shorts and Reeboks, insistent that Elise discard sandals for Reeboks too—an action which set the butterflies inside her stomach fluttering into a nervous dance as he hunkered down to effect the change.

It was a glorious afternoon, the sun's summer warmth caressing her skin as they wandered slowly along the hard-packed sand, which was still slightly damp from an outgoing tide. A gentle breeze teased the length of her hair, causing a few tendrils to drift across her cheek.

There was a sense of freedom apparent, a lightness resulting from confinement in hospital for the past ten days, and she allowed herself several shallow breaths in order to drink in the salty smell of the ocean, the cleanliness of unpolluted air.

A few children were at play in the distance, their chatter and laughter barely audible as they darted back and forth, heads bent in their quest for seashells.

It was good to be alive, Elise decided with a slight smile, only to have the smile slowly fade with the realisation that, had Fate been unkind, her loss would have included the right to life of her unborn child.

An arm curved lightly round her waist, and she turned towards him, her eyes wide as she searched his strong, firmly etched features.

Some degree of her inner anguish must have been apparent, for his hold tightened fractionally, and his lips brushed the top of her head.

She was supremely conscious of his close proximity, aware of his warmth, and the security his powerful frame afforded.

They continued walking until Alejandro drew to a halt. 'This is far enough, I think.'

Elise viewed the short distance they had travelled and wrinkled her nose at him. 'I feel fine,' she protested, not wanting to return to the house just yet. 'Look,' she exclaimed, as a large golden retriever loped along the water's edge. 'Isn't he beautiful?' The dog's movements were poetry in motion, measured lolloping strides that sent his long golden hair flowing back from his young body.

'Beautiful,' Alejandro agreed, and when she turned towards him she saw his focus was centred on her, not the dog.

The breath caught in her throat, and for several long seconds her eyes felt impossibly large, then she smiled, a tinge of humour lifting the edges of her generous mouth. 'I don't suppose I could persuade you to walk a bit further?'

'No,' he refused lazily, and his eyes held amusement as he looked down into her upturned features.

'So, this is it for today?'

'Don't sound so disappointed.' He lifted a hand and tucked a flyaway lock of hair behind her ear. 'There's always tomorrow.'

Without a word she turned slowly and walked back to the house at his side. Once indoors, he led the way through the kitchen. It was warm, and she felt in need of a long, refreshing drink. She watched as he extracted two glasses, filled each with fruit juice, and held one out to her.

'You have enjoyed your taste of fresh air and sunshine?'

'I don't think anyone fully appreciates the choice of freedom to move anywhere at will until that choice is removed.' She lifted the glass and took a long swallow of the icy liquid, watching as he followed her actions.

There were several chairs and two sun-loungers positioned on the wide, partly covered terrace, and Elise moved outdoors and sank gratefully into one of the loungers. The sun was beginning to lose some of its warmth, although the house provided sufficient protection from the breeze to make sitting outdoors a pleasure.

'Your face has regained a little colour,' Alejandro observed as he chose the other lounger close by, and she bore his scrutiny with equanimity.

'Another two weeks of this, and I'll resemble a sybarite,' she said, with a tinge of humour.

'Your welfare is very important to me.'

The quietly spoken words stirred her sensitised nerve-ends, and she examined his features carefully. 'I hesitate to think at what cost,' she ventured slowly.

Something flickered in the depths of his eyes, a fleeting emotion she was unable to define before it was successfully hidden. 'I retain eminently qualified personnel.'

Whose positions within the Santanas corporation Alejandro would instantly terminate should any one of them fail him in any way. The knowledge was an instinctive judgement that needed no qualification, and she was silent for several long minutes.

'It's difficult to comprehend that there was a time when I knew everything about you,' Elise confessed.

'While now there are only gaps?'

'A deep, yawning abyss,' she corrected with a faint grimace.

'Which you would like me to fill?'

'You did that to some extent while I was in hospital.' Details, facts. Not the personal things she desperately wanted to know.

'So, *querida*,' he mocked gently, searching her intent expression, 'where would you like me to begin?'

'I think...with you. Where you were born, when. Your family. Things you enjoy doing.'

'An extended biography?'

'The condensed version.'

His eyes held warm humour, and his soft laughter transformed the hard-chiselled bone-structure, so that for a brief moment he appeared almost human, she decided, as he lifted the glass to his lips and drained the contents in one easy swallow.

'My father was born in Andalucía, the son of a wealthy landowner. My mother was a descendant of the French aristocracy. After their marriage they emigrated to Australia, where I was born. A year later my mother died in childbirth. Papa never fully recovered emotionally, and my paternal grandmother flew out for an extended visit, only to stay on and raise her only grandson. It was because of that good woman's determined strength that I

stayed at school and received the education my
father insisted I endure.'

He paused to shoot her a faintly whimsical smile.
'I was known to display rebellion on occasion.'

Elise had a vivid mental picture of a tall youth
whose broad bone-structure had yet to acquire its
measure of adult musculature.

'At university I acquired several degrees asso-
ciated with business management and became part
of my father's financial empire. At the lowest level,'
Alejandro qualified drily. 'A Santanas son was accorded few advantages, and I spent several years
proving my worth. A fatal accident ended my
father's life, and I was catapulted through the ranks
to a position on the board of directors.' He spared
her a faintly cynical glance. 'The next few years
were—difficult, shall we say? Men with years of
experience do not view kindly a young man taking
control of a string of multinational companies, or
making decisions that oppose their way of thinking.'

Elise looked at him thoughtfully, seeing the
strength of purpose, the chilling degree of hardness
apparent, and barely controlled the faint shiver that
threatened to slither down her spine. 'You succeeded.' As if there could be any doubt.

His expression did not alter for several long seconds. 'Yes,' he acknowledged with wry cynicism.

Had she been his social equal? Somehow she
didn't think so.

'I have little idea of what my childhood was like,'
she proffered with pensive introspection. 'The
photo albums you brought to the hospital reveal

events of which I have no recollection. I can only piece together the visual impression of a happy childhood. A mother I can't remember, whose passing must surely have caused my father great grief. I don't even know the extent to which I missed her. Or whether boarding-school was a happy experience or a lonely one.' She paused, her eyes dark with reflected intensity. 'I chose paediatric nursing as a career, but I don't know if I had a boyfriend, or several. Or what sort of life I led before I met you.'

'I doubt the existence of many boyfriends in other than a platonic sense,' Alejandro put in with indolent humour. 'You were relatively inexperienced.'

Her eyes sparked with resentful resignation. 'A fact you no doubt soon remedied.'

His husky laughter was almost her undoing. 'With immense pleasure, *mi mujer*. You proved to be an apt and willing pupil.' He leaned forward and brushed his mouth against her own, his eyes gleaming with humour as she reared back from his touch. 'Time to prepare dinner, I think.'

An hour later they sat down to soup, and followed it with grilled steak and salad, electing to watch television until Alejandro deemed it time to retire to bed.

Elise had little option but to accept his assistance, and she stood, head bent, lower lip caught between her teeth, as he began freeing her clothes.

There was something incredibly sensual in having him tend to the buttons on her blouse, the fleeting touch of his warm fingers as they brushed her sensitised flesh. To have him unclip her bra and feel his light touch against each breast.

Last night should have prepared her for the protracted intimacy of standing part-naked in front of him. Yet, try as she might, she was unable to control the shallowness of her breathing, or prevent the faint colour heightening her cheekbones.

It was a relief to escape into the *en suite* bathroom and shower alone, and she took as long as she dared before emerging to find Alejandro waiting to towel her dry.

She wanted to say she could manage, and for a moment she almost did, but one look at his dark, brooding features was sufficient for her to realise that such an action would be the height of foolishness.

The instant her nightgown was safely in place she made to turn away, only to have her movement stalled as her chin was caught between a firm thumb and forefinger.

'*Don't*,' Alejandro began in cautionary remonstrance, 'erect obstacles where none exist.'

The soft drawl matched the faint mockery evident in those dark eyes, and a lump rose in her throat that made it difficult for her to swallow.

Her mouth trembled, and she felt the ache of unshed tears as she searched the strong masculine features, noting the grooves that slashed his cheeks and the tiny lines fanning out from the corners of his eyes.

'How can you say that?' she queried in strangled tones, feeling at a loss to cope with the force of his compelling masculinity.

He lifted a hand and traced a finger down the slope of her nose, then traversed the tip to settle on the curve of her lip.

'Easily,' Alejandro assured her as he lightly stroked the soft fullness of the lower contour before exploring the generous line above.

His touch was provocative, light, and sent warning flares to each separate nerve-ending as a deliciously warm sensation slowly radiated through her whole body.

I could close my eyes and become lost, thought Elise, swayed by emotion and held in its invasive thrall. There was a part of her that hungered for the touch of his hands, his mouth, and she had the most insane desire to plead with him to turn the erotic images into reality.

A soft moan whispered from her throat as his mouth closed over hers, teasing, tasting, in a gentle exploration that brought her body close to his in an involuntary movement as he carefully deepened the kiss.

It was heaven, she decided hazily, filled with such agonising sweetness that she felt as if she were melting, boneless. *His*.

She wanted more than the mere fusing of their mouths. Much more. It was almost as if some secret part of her was privy to a knowledge that eluded her conscious mind, and she gave a tiny despairing moan as his tongue slowed its masterful stroking dance with her own as a prelude to retreat.

As he lifted his head her eyes clung to his, wide and almost trance-like, for several long seconds before his features swam into focus.

Elise glimpsed the passion held severely in check, the deep slumbering emotion that darkened his gaze, and something else she couldn't quite define.

Her lips were swollen and the inside of her mouth so acutely sensitised that she wondered if she was capable of uttering so much as a word.

Never had she felt so hauntingly vulnerable, or so fragile. A pulse thudded visibly at the edge of her throat as the blood drummed through her veins and she lifted her left hand, only to let it fall helplessly to her side.

'Bed, I think,' Alejandro decreed, his eyes narrowing as he glimpsed the effort it cost her to retain some measure of control.

His hand cupped her left shoulder, then slid to her breast, slipping beneath the silk to shape the tumescent mound with exquisite care.

She felt it swell beneath his touch, the peak tautening in sensitive arousal, then his mouth assumed a wry humorous twist as he lifted both hands to frame her face.

'Television, or would you prefer to read?'

It took considerable effort to summon a faint smile as she allowed him to lead her towards the bed. 'Television,' she declared unevenly. 'Providing I get to choose the programme.'

'Brave words, *querida*,' he teased lightly. 'You will probably be asleep by the time I have shaved and showered.'

She was unable to still the faint fluttering of butterfly wings inside her stomach, and her gaze became pensive as he stripped down to his briefs, then crossed to the *en suite* bathroom.

He was an enigma, Elise decided thoughtfully as she endeavoured to concentrate on the images flickering across the screen.

Darkly intense, almost frightening. Yet he could be gentle and considerate. A difficult mixture to comprehend, she accepted silently, wondering if there had ever been a time when she had understood him.

Thinking about it made her tired, and her lashes drifted down as she lapsed into dreamless oblivion.

CHAPTER FOUR

THE days ran one into the other, each following a similar pattern to the one preceding it. They rose early, dressed, and went for a walk along the deserted beach, then returned to eat a simple breakfast out on the covered terrace, after which Alejandro would disappear into the study for an hour.

It was his only concession to maintaining a check on business interests, and although there was a phone in the car, and a mobile cellular unit tucked into the pocket of his shorts whenever they moved away from the house, only once did either ring. His instructions on each occasion had been chillingly brief.

Occasionally he would pack a picnic lunch and drive to one of the neighbouring beaches, or a designated park. Sometimes they stayed at home and watched videos. Late each afternoon they embarked on a leisurely walk along the beach.

With every passing day the pain in Elise's hand lessened, the bruising faded, and she was soon able to don and shed her clothes without help, something she considered to be a milestone.

Alejandro appeared to be attuned to her every mood, watchful that she didn't become tired, and able to coax her into laughter with very little effort.

at all, until gradually she began to relax and regard him with hesitant affection.

She became accustomed to the light brush of his fingers across her skin, the touch of his hand on her arm, cupping her shoulder, resting at the small of her back or curved round her waist. The light touch of his mouth against her own was something else, and more than once she was barely able to suppress a tide of sensation as he instigated a teasing kiss. At night she no longer felt uneasy when he joined her in bed, nor did she attempt to pull her hand away when he threaded his fingers through her own.

Yet all the time she was aware of his restraint, the latent passion just beneath the surface of his control. Occasionally she glimpsed evidence of it in the darkening of his eyes, felt it in the sudden quickening of his pulse.

The knowledge made her nervous, tugging at something hidden deep inside her. It generated a waiting expectancy that sent tiny flares of fire surging through her veins, set her fine body-hair on edge, and curled insidiously at the core of her femininity.

The weekend came and went, with a series of scattered showers which kept them indoors. Monday dawned fresh and clear, with not a cloud in sight.

'I thought we'd pack some food in the car and head north,' Alejandro declared as she cleared the last of their breakfast dishes and watched as he rinsed and slotted them into the dishwasher.

'What time do you want to leave?' Elise queried with an alacrity that curved his mouth into a slow teasing smile.

'Allow me an hour in the study. Around ten.'

It was a glorious day, the sun high in an azure sky, with a soft breeze tempering the midsummer heat.

Alejandro brought the car to a halt and switched off the engine. The view out over the park was one of tranquillity, with several large trees lining the grassed verge. Bleached white sand bordered the eastern boundary, and the surface of the lazy out-going ocean tide shimmered in the early afternoon heat.

'Hungry?'

Elise turned towards him and offered an easy smile. 'Ravenous.'

The park was almost empty, and Alejandro slid from behind the wheel and walked to the rear of the vehicle to retrieve a rug, cushions and a picnic hamper from the capacious boot, choosing a smooth patch of grass beneath a nearby tree.

Minutes later Elise sank to her knees and watched as he began apportioning food on to two plates.

Cold chicken and salad, with crusty bread rolls and fresh fruit, presented a veritable feast, and she picked up a chicken leg and bit into it with relish.

'Your appetite is improving,' Alejandro commented in approval, and she wrinkled her nose at him.

He sat stretched out beside her, his powerfully muscled legs tanned by the sun. His feet, like hers, were shod in Reeboks.

Looking the antithesis of a wheeling, dealing multinational corporate leader, he had ignored designer leisurewear in favour of cut-off jeans and a loose cotton shirt. The effect was devastating, she conceded as she allowed herself a circumspect appraisal, all too aware of the effect he had on her equilibrium as she admired his chiselled jaw, the firm sensual mouth, then slowly raised her eyes to meet the dark intentness of his gaze.

There was a latent indolence apparent, a studied watchfulness that was wholly sexual. She could sense his potent chemistry, like a magnetic force field, and something stirred deep within, pulsing through the tracery of veins, triggering nerve-ends until her whole body became caught up in the thrall of physical awareness.

'A sip of wine?'

'It will make me sleepy,' she protested as he extended the patterned flute to her lips. There was something incredibly intimate about placing her mouth to the rim where his had been only seconds before, and she savoured a small quantity of the excellent Chardonnay, letting it slip slowly down her throat, then followed it with several long swallows of iced water.

'Would that be such a bad thing?'

She sensed the faint humour in his voice and her eyes widened slightly. It would be so easy to reach out and touch him, to place fingers against that hard jaw and explore the vertical crease slashing each cheek. She wanted to, badly.

Almost as much as she wanted to feel his mouth against her own, his hand shaping her breast. A long, slow prelude to a passionate overture. Except that she wasn't sure if she was ready for the finale.

Such wayward thoughts were infinitely dangerous to her peace of mind. In an effort to shut them out she turned her attention to the horizon, aware of his deft movements as he extracted a fresh peach and began peeling it.

What was he like as a lover? Passionate, primitive, *shameless*. Dear Lord in heaven, could there be any doubt?

'Elise?'

She turned at the sound of his voice, and her fingers shook slightly as she took a segment of fruit from his outstretched hand. 'Thanks.'

It was deliciously cool and juicy, and she followed it with a glass of chilled mineral water.

If she lay back and closed her eyes, maybe it would stem this inner restlessness. She hadn't taken into account the soft sea breeze, the sun's warmth, or their midday meal. Together they had a soporific effect, and it took only minutes for her to slip into a light doze.

Elise woke slowly, passing through the threshold of sleep to a state of nebulous consciousness, aware that the slight feeling of lethargy had dissipated. It was difficult to tell whether it could be attributed to the recuperation process or her pregnancy.

Perhaps it was a combination of both, she decided lazily as she let her eyelashes sweep slowly upwards.

Alejandro lay sprawled in a half sitting position within touching distance, his head propped in one hand as he faced her, and she blinked as he lifted a hand and trailed gentle fingers down the edge of her jaw.

'Pleasant dreams?'

She couldn't recollect even one. 'How long have I been asleep?'

'Almost an hour,' he responded, and her eyes widened in disbelief.

'You should have woken me.'

'Why?' he asked, watching the play of emotions across her expressive features. 'There's no need to hurry home.'

Elise stared at him, aware of the sheer physicality of his powerful body and his ability to make her feel infinitely fragile. There was a warmth evident in those dark eyes, a latent sensuality that was deeply disturbing.

It was as if she was being drawn to him by some invisible magnet, and she became increasingly confused as her emotions swung like a pendulum between cautious acceptance and denial.

Logic reasoned that a man of his considerable means could easily have hired a nurse-companion for her and continued to devote most of his energies to an extensive business empire. Yet he had not chosen to delegate. Surely such an action was sufficient evidence of his caring? Why this instinctive niggling doubt that persisted despite every effort to rationalise and dispel it?

'Ready for some exercise?'

Her eyes cleared, and a smile curved her mouth. 'Yes.'

With easy lithe movements he rose to his feet, extending a hand to help her, then he stowed the hamper in the boot and followed it with the rug and cushions.

They walked in companionable silence, and Elise lifted her face to the sunshine, loving the soft afternoon breeze as it came off the sea, the slight tangy smell of salt refreshingly evident.

There were young children playing close by, three beneath the age of five, and a lovely plump baby sitting on a rug beneath the shade of a wide beach-umbrella.

Elise looked at the baby's bright eyes, the wide smile and happily flailing arms as the young mother deftly exchanged one nappy for another.

Something tugged deep inside her, a wistful longing that came from nowhere, and she made no protest as Alejandro curved an arm around her waist and pulled her close to his side.

Unbidden, her own fingers traced a light path across her waist, then paused in an unconsciously protective gesture.

Would their child be a dark-haired imp inheriting his father's genes, or a flaxen-haired angel who would steal her father's heart? Without doubt their child would be fortunate enough to lead a privileged existence.

It was late afternoon when they arrived back at Palm Beach, and Elise wandered through the house while Alejandro checked the fax machine and made a few calls.

She found her way into the informal lounge and picked up the remote control unit, flicking from one television channel to another in a bid to discover something worthy of her attention. At this time of the afternoon most of the programmes were designed to educate or amuse children, and she discarded the unit in favour of a magazine.

'Would you like to eat out? There's a variety of restaurants within a short driving distance.'

Alejandro's entry into the room had been soundless, and she glanced up in surprise as he crossed to stand within touching distance.

In public? The idea held definite appeal. '*Yes.*'

His soft laughter held a degree of quizzical warmth, and she swallowed convulsively as he caught hold of her hand and lifted it to his lips, kissing each finger in turn before slipping inward to caress the softness of her palm. The sensation sent tiny shock-waves radiating from her feminine core, and she shivered at the lambent warmth evident in those dark eyes so close to her own.

Releasing her, he slid both hands beneath her blouse to free the fastening of her bra. His fingers were warm, his touch deft, unleashing a number of sensations she found difficult to ignore.

It would have been all too easy to lift a hand and pull his head down to hers to initiate a long, sweet kiss. Except that if she did, it wouldn't stop there.

'If you continue to look at me like that for much longer,' Alejandro drawled, pressing a finger to the soft lower fullness of her lip, 'I'll take it as an invitation to join you in the shower. Afterwards,' he promised huskily, 'where and when we eat won't be a consideration.'

Colour stained her cheekbones and she turned away from him, forcing herself to walk to their suite with unhurried steps. Once there, she gathered up fresh underwear and entered the bathroom.

The water's warm spray soothed her fractured nerves, and she stayed longer than necessary, emerging to towel herself dry, then don lace-edged briefs.

Alejandro was in the process of tucking a shirt into his trousers when she entered the bedroom, and she consciously averted her gaze as she crossed to the capacious wardrobe to select something suitable to wear.

Black silk culottes, slim-heeled black sandals, and a long white sleeveless button-through silk top, she decided as she extracted the clothes from their hangers. It was a go-anywhere ensemble that was both comfortable and elegant.

Elise stepped into the culottes and pulled them into position at her waist, then reached for the top as Alejandro crossed to her side.

'No bra to fasten?'

'The top is fully lined,' she explained, intent on closing the buttons. She lifted her head and her eyes clashed with his dark, disturbing gaze. A spiral of sensation began in the region of her stomach, radiating a wealth of sensual warmth which she found difficult to ignore. Dampening it down, she forced her voice to remain steady. 'I won't be long. I just need to brush my hair and apply basic make-up.'

'You look about sixteen.'

She managed a shaky smile. 'Much too young to be married and pregnant to a man like you.'

'*Por Dios*,' Alejandro drawled. 'Why a man like me?'

Levity, surely, was an appropriate weapon, and she used it without hesitation. 'If you're going to swear, at least do so in English,' she chastised with mock severity.

He laughed softly and brushed his lips against hers. 'You *are* beginning to recover,' he mocked drily. 'Soon you'll be challenging me at every turn.'

Dear heaven. She'd been that brave to cross verbal swords with him ... that *foolish*?

'If you're ready,' he suggested easily, 'let's go and eat.'

She moved into the bathroom, brushed her hair until it resembled a curtain of pale silk, stroked translucent gold shadow on to each eyelid, then applied lipliner and gloss.

When she emerged Alejandro was waiting for her, an impeccably tailored reefer jacket lending an air of sophistication she felt at a loss to match.

The restaurant he chose was Italian, small, delightfully intimate and filled with a variety of beguiling aromas that teased her taste-buds. There was also a tiny square of parquet floor and a man of middle years playing a soft romantic ballad on a small electronic keyboard.

Elise ordered tortellini with mushrooms served with garlic bread, while Alejandro opted for pasta with a marinara sauce, and afterwards she sat back feeling replete.

'Dessert?'

She shook her head. 'I couldn't fit in another mouthful.'

He seemed totally at ease, and she couldn't help being aware that his presence caused a flutter of interest among several of the female patrons.

How could she blame them? He was a superb male animal, who possessed more than his share of sexual magnetism. Inherent good looks and an overwhelming aura of power made him a spell-binding challenge few women could ignore.

The lilting music and warm convivial atmos-phere of the restaurant were persuasive, and she cast him a faintly wistful smile.

'Would you like to try the dance-floor?'

She looked helplessly at the small square of par-quetry that held one couple, then inclined her head in silent acquiescence.

Minutes later she wasn't so sure it was a good idea. Her right hand lay supported between her breasts, while the fingers of her left hand rested against his shoulder. His hands were loosely linked behind her hips, forming a protective cage, and this close she could sense his body-warmth beneath the sophisticated mantle of his clothes.

His movements were sure, fluid, his strength a potent entity as he guided her with effortless ease. The keyboard player sang a hauntingly slow ballad, and to her surprise her steps didn't falter once, although her breathing quickened in tempo with her fast-beating pulse.

Warm heat spread through her veins, suffusing her body until she was aware of every sensory pleasure-spot, and a deep aching need that cried out for his touch.

She felt his hands shift to curve over the slight swell of her bottom as the ballad finished and another began, even more poignant than the last. Seconds later, she felt the brush of his lips against her hair as they trailed down to settle at her temple, and her stomach executed a tiny somersault, then went into a series of crazy flips as his warm breath stirred a few stray tendrils close to her ear.

Slowly she lifted her head, her eyes skimming the broad column of his throat to take in the firm contours of his mouth, the straight patrician nose, the sculpted cheekbones, and lastly his intensely dark eyes.

What she glimpsed there deepened the colour already staining her cheeks, and her mouth trembled slightly as she sought to put some distance between them.

He immediately loosened his hold, allowing one arm to curve lightly round her back as he led her from the floor.

'Another drink?' Alejandro queried when they were seated.

Something cool, *icy*, she qualified silently. 'Please,' she accepted. 'Lemonade with a dash of lime.'

He ordered coffee for himself, and she sipped the contents of her glass, contrarily wanting the evening to be over, yet strangely hesitant to leave the restaurant.

Why so apprehensive? she reiterated to herself as the Bentley cruised smoothly towards Palm Beach. There was no medical reason why they shouldn't resume intimacy, and to be so racked with nerves was ridiculous.

'Do you want to share?'

The sound of his voice startled her, and she turned towards him in silent query.

'Your thoughts,' Alejandro elaborated as he eased the large vehicle into the driveway, then activated the remote control to raise the garage doors.

Dear heaven, had he guessed? What would he say if she said she was scared stiff... of *him* in the role of lover? More than likely he would be mildly amused, she decided wretchedly.

As soon as the car came to a halt she released the seatbelt and slid to her feet, waiting as he sprang the locking system before crossing to her side as they entered the house.

Once indoors she made straight for the stairs, only to come to an abrupt halt as his hand closed over her elbow and he turned her round to face him.

His eyes were faintly hooded, his tone a deceptively soft drawl. 'You're reacting like a skittish kitten, unsure whether to leap and run, or stay.'

'Perhaps because that's how I feel.'

'You find my touch abhorrent?'

Oh, my, nothing like aiming straight for the jugular. 'No,' she disclaimed quietly. 'But I'm not ready to sleep with you.'

'We already sleep together.' His voice was so dangerously quiet that it sent an icy shiver scudding down her back.

Dull pink streaked her cheeks. He was fully aware of the havoc he was creating, and she hated him for the deliberate assault on her ambivalent emotions.

'You know that isn't what I meant.'

He caught hold of her chin between thumb and forefinger, tilting it so that she had to look at him.

She couldn't articulate a single word, and it was difficult to swallow the lump that had suddenly risen in her throat. Her eyes felt large and impossibly wide as she watched his head descend, and she was incapable of movement as he angled his mouth to settle over hers in a kiss that claimed his possession, savouring it in a manner that alternated between gentleness and restrained savagery.

Elise told herself she should be shocked. Instead, she became caught up in a tide of deep primitive need.

One hand cradled her face, the other cupped her bottom as he pulled her hard against him. Evidence of his arousal was a hard, throbbing entity, and she gave a faint moan of protest as his mouth took on a light teasing quality, then slowly withdrew.

She could only look at him, totally ignorant of the deep slumberous quality evident in her eyes. Her lips felt swollen, and she could have sworn they trembled beneath the intentness of his dark gaze.

It was as if time stood still, for she wasn't conscious of anything except the man: his eyes, the sensual curve of his mouth, the hard planes of his jaw, the strength of his chin, the texture of his skin.

He didn't say a word for what seemed an age, then he leaned forward, swept an arm beneath her knees and lifted her against his chest.

Sensation curled deep inside her stomach and began radiating through her body as he mounted the stairs to the upper floor.

On entering their suite he closed the door, slid off her shoes, then carefully set her down on her feet. Lifting a hand, he slowly traced the contours of her mouth, probing the softness with a gentleness that made her catch her breath.

'I want to make love with you.'

Her eyes dilated and her pulse began to kick in a quickened beat. She wanted to voice her nervousness, but the words never left her lips.

His eyes held hers as he shrugged off his jacket and tossed it over a chair, then he loosened his tie and discarded it before unfastening the buttons on his shirt. Next came his shoes and socks.

Elise couldn't look away as his fingers unbuckled his belt, slid free the slim metal clasp, then freed the zip on his trousers.

Black silk briefs rode low on his hips, barely containing the turgid rigidity of his manhood, and awareness arrowed from her feminine core, focused and so intense that she was unable to suppress a slight shiver that spiralled down her spine.

Slowly he closed the distance between them, took her left hand in his, and led her to the bed. His touch was warm and strong, and she uttered no protest as he sat on the mattress's edge and drew her close.

Her eyes were almost on a level with his, and she felt mesmerised by the dark gleaming passion evident as he lifted a hand and lightly traced the contours of her face.

The touch of his fingers against her skin was electric, and she swallowed convulsively as they trailed down the column of her throat and traversed a path to the edge of her top.

He freed one button, then the next, until the edges hung loose, and she uttered a faint gasp as he brushed the full curve of her breast.

'The thought of doing this has driven me to edge of sanity,' Alejandro said huskily. 'All evening, every movement you made emphasised their unfettered state.' With extreme care he eased the blouse free and tossed it to join his discarded clothes.

'Beautiful,' he whispered, gently shaping the creamy fullness, testing its weight as he lightly circled each sensitised peak.

Acute sensation curled deeply inside her stomach, and her throat began to constrict as he leaned forward and took one peak into his mouth, rolling it with the roughened edge of his tongue until she felt it swell and harden beneath his touch.

A low groan locked in her throat as he bestowed a similar attention on its twin. Then she gasped out loud as he began to suckle deeply, drawing from each tender peak an erotic satisfaction she had no conscious urge to deny.

When at last he lifted his head, she met his gaze through half closed lids, and she stood quite still as he reached for the waistband of her culottes and began easing the silk down over her hips to pool at her feet. Satin and lace briefs followed, and she felt heat sear her body as he conducted a leisurely appraisal.

He lifted a hand and trailed gentle fingers up over her ribcage, then slowly traversed her hip, slipping to caress the slight roundness of her bottom before brushing a path to her thigh.

His eyes never left hers, and Elise felt her own dilate as he sought the soft, curling hair, then followed its upper line, caressing, moving back and forth, until her whole body began to sing like a finely tuned instrument.

Slowly his hand lowered until he reached the junction between her thighs, and she uttered an audible gasp as he initiated an intimate exploration she was hesitant to accept.

'Am I frightening you, *querida*?'

Fear wasn't quite the word she would have used to describe her feelings. Excitement, exultation, to name only two. 'No.' The single negation emerged as a whispered gasp.

His touch proved an erotic torture, and she shuddered as an initial spasm caught hold of her and spiralled out of control.

'Alejandro.' His name on her lips was a deep, husky groan.

Dear God, such sweet magic. It was like being taken straight to heaven and shown a hundred different delights.

'Gently, *querida*,' he cautioned as she reached blindly for him.

The soft sounds emerging from her throat were incomprehensible, and she was hardly aware of him easing her down on to the bed.

He carefully moved her injured hand into a comfortable position, then stretched out at her side.

His mouth sought hers in a long, slow, drugging kiss that alternately teased and tantalised, and she began to tremble as his lips began a path of erotic discovery so that it was all she could do not to cry out as he nuzzled the entry to her innermost core.

Brazen, she admitted silently as she climbed to dizzying heights. Shameless. Hopelessly, helplessly passionate and disruptively sensual. She never wanted it to end, yet the spiral of sensation was so incredibly acute she wasn't sure how much longer she could maintain any restraint.

It was the most intimate kiss of all, a deep, drugging oral simulation of the sexual act. A sensual gift so exquisite, so incredibly generous that she wanted to weep from the joy of it.

Slowly his head moved, and he began raining a trail of open-mouthed kisses over the plane of her stomach, upwards to caress the soft underswell of each breast before fastening on one sensitised peak.

Then he raised his head to look down at her, taking in the slumberous darkness of her eyes, the soft pink that coloured her pale features, and her parted lips.

Elise lifted a tentative hand to the dark springy mat of hair on his chest, and she traced his shoulder, played delicately with the strong cage of his ribs before moving involuntarily down to the taut flat planes of his stomach.

She felt the muscles clench, and unconsciously her tongue edged out and ran a tentative path along her lower lip.

'*Dios*,' Alejandro cursed in husky remonstrance. 'If you don't stop *now*, I will pass the limit of my control.'

She looked at him carefully and glimpsed the latent passion, the heated desire barely masked.

A feeling of power raced through her veins, building until she felt like a goddess in charge of something so infinitely precious, so rare that only *she* could grant him the release he sought.

With deliberate slowness she trailed her fingers to trace the length of his distended shaft. Fascinated, she afforded it a gentle tactile exploration, feeling it engorge further beneath her featherlight touch.

'I don't want your control.' Her voice was a husky enticement, and she heard his deep despairing groan followed by the sound of silk being torn from hair-roughened skin.

'Dear God,' he responded piously, 'I doubt you would condone my lack of it.'

With extreme care he prepared her to accept him, and she arched instinctively, welcoming the intrusion as he gained entry. The feeling was intense as moist tissues stretched to accommodate his length, and she exulted in the total enclosure.

It was almost as if this were their first time together, and she experienced a sense of wonder in his possession.

As crazy as it seemed, she could *feel* the blood vessels engorge as she encased him, the spasmodic action of inner muscles as they sought to encourage and match his rhythm.

It was almost as if her body recognised what her conscious mind was reluctant to accept, urging a blatant display of passion that was vaguely shocking.

With the grace of an uninhibited Circe she traced the length of his spine, then gently kneaded his tightly muscled flank. Almost of their own volition her fingers trailed to his hip, then began a slow exploratory inner path to the highly sensitised base of his sex.

Gently, very gently she squeezed the sensitive glans, and exulted in his indrawn breath. Not content, she initiated a seeking path with her lips until they discovered a sensitive male nipple, and she suckled shamelessly, nipping occasionally with her teeth until she felt his powerful body shudder in the initial throes of sensual ecstasy.

She wanted . . . Dear heaven, what *did* she want? More, *more* than this carefully controlled pacing. All of him, plunging deep inside her in a torrent of wild strokes that would take them both to the heights.

Elise was hardly conscious of the soft sounds emerging from her throat as her body reacted with instinctive ease, lifting, angling with a will of its own as she intuitively matched each and every one of his movements.

His hands on either side of her shoulders braced his weight, and she met his mouth hungrily as it closed over hers, his kiss so deep, so consummate, it mirrored the sexual act itself in an erotic joining that culminated in a wild journey to the centre of her sensual universe.

Her mind might deny any conscious acknowledgement of her primeval soul, but every sensitive chord in her awakened body was attuned to this one man, honed by his expertise, tutored with a mesmeric passion that surpassed every restrictive boundary.

There could be no vestige of doubt that she was *his*. The traitorous proof was apparent in every sensitive nerve-ending, the acute vibrancy that thrummed through her veins, heating her blood to a fervent flame of desire that could only lead to a conflagration of all the senses. *Passion*—pagan, primitive, and wildly erotic.

When it was finally over, she was so emotionally enervated that she doubted her ability to move so much as a muscle.

She felt tinglingly alive, as if every nerve-ending had become acutely sensitised by his touch, yet drowsy and deliciously spent. Languid, she corrected, smiling as she felt his lips caress the curve of her neck, then slip down to bestow an open-mouthed kiss on each breast in turn.

He was...magnificent, she acknowledged dreamily. A tender lover, caring, considerate of her needs. Had *he* enjoyed himself with her as much as she had with him? Was he satisfied, complete? Somehow she couldn't bring herself to ask.

She felt him move, and she shifted her head to look at him as he retrieved the support for her arm and carefully fixed it in place.

His eyes were dark, slumberous, and her own skittered to a point somewhere beyond his left shoulder.

'Don't,' Alejandro chided huskily as he cradled her head and forced her to look at him, 'attempt to hide what was an intensely beautiful experience for both of us.' His thumb probed the swollen softness of her mouth. *'Exquisito.'*

He slid down to lie beside her, gathering her close so that her head nestled beneath his shoulder. With minimum effort he caught hold of the sheet and drew it over them. 'Go to sleep, *querida*,' he bade her gently.

Yet she couldn't, not for a long time. Instead she lay still, listening to the steady beat of his heart.

Had it always been like this, right from the beginning? Or had it taken time and practice to reach such a pinnacle of sexual satisfaction?

Sadly, she didn't know. There was just the aching acceptance that her body remembered what her mind could not.

CHAPTER FIVE

THE beach was peaceful, with the merest breeze slipping in from the ocean to caress Elise's skin and tease the length of her hair.

The water was a deep blue, its surface smooth in the distance, cresting as it neared the shore to swirl foam-laced over the hard-packed sand.

A strange feeling of ambivalence held her in its spell...and a degree of sadness. She felt safe here. Secure.

The past ten days had been idyllic: lazily spent sunshine-filled days and easy companionship, long moonlit nights and gentle loving.

Tomorrow they were to return to Point Piper. Next week she was to begin physiotherapy, and there were appointments with the obstetrician and neurologist. Within a very short time Alejandro would drive into the city each morning to spend most of each day in his office atop one of Sydney's inner-city modern architectural masterpieces, and she would be alone...

An office. Atop a modern city architect-designed building...

She saw it clearly.

A large, sumptuously furnished room, clean lines, expensive prints on the walls, and a wide expanse of tinted plate glass with splendid views over the city and harbour.

An encapsulated vision of a room with a tall, broad-framed figure leaning against the edge of a large executive desk. Alejandro, his expression harsh and forbidding, his silent anger a vivid entity.

She was there, recapturing her anger... his. Hearing the words with frightening clarity.

'My respect for your father,' Alejandro declared in a dangerously soft, slightly accented voice that was chilling in its intensity, 'allowed you to get past my secretary and buy five minutes of my valuable time.' Dark eyes became icily dispassionate. 'I suggest you make good use of it.'

'My father doesn't know I've initiated a personal appeal,' Elise assured him in immediate defence.

'It makes no difference. My decision is irrevocable.'

The words were clipped, hard, and horribly final. 'How can you say that?' she demanded, launching into passionate speech. 'He deserves——'

'Another chance?'

'Why don't you let me finish a sentence?' she parried with mounting antipathy, and encountered his visible cynicism.

'Four minutes and thirty seconds doesn't allow for verbose explanation.'

She wanted to hit him. She almost did. Yet there was something electrifyingly primitive beneath his sophisticated façade that warned her that he would retaliate in kind without the slightest qualm.

'Without your help, my father faces bankruptcy,' she enlightened him starkly, and glimpsed no visible change in his expression.

'I head a multinational corporation which has a complex variety of investments throughout the world. Although I retain a controlling percentage, as director I am responsible to a number of shareholders. Your father's latest appeal for a further extension resulted in extensive feasibility studies. The findings negate any possibility of directorial board approval for either an increase in borrowings or an extension of time.'

Elise felt her misgivings increase at his inflexibility. 'He's ill,' she stressed with a sense of desperation. 'Conclusive tests reveal the necessity for heart surgery.'

'I cannot gamble with my shareholders' money.'

The hard unyielding words brought a rush of anger she barely managed to contain. Don't blow it, an inner voice cautioned. 'My father is a very proud man for whom honesty and integrity are sacrosanct. Hansen Holdings has been a family company for three generations,' she informed him with commendable steadiness, given the short rein she held on her temper. 'It will kill him if he loses everything in a bankruptcy action.'

His expression did not change. He was a superb tactician, watchful, waiting for her to plot the next move. There was no doubt he would win the game, but for the moment she was still a player, even if he held all the cards.

'Commendable sentiment isn't sufficient reason for me to grant the extension your father requires.'

He was an obdurate, unfeeling monster, she decided with bitter acrimony. Truly *el diablo*. Pride lifted her chin and lent her eyes a fiery sparkle. 'What would you consider to be sufficient reason?'

His eyes darkened fractionally, and she was unable to look away. His intent gaze had a mesmeric effect, and a slow heat suffused her body, reaching deep to unleash an entire gamut of sensations she was loath to recognise.

A deep insistent burr was almost an anticlimax as it broke the fraught silence, and Elise watched as he reached for the in-house phone, privy to the brusqueness of his voice as he checked the time and intimated he was on his way.

Replacing the receiver, he moved away from the desk. 'I am needed in the board room.'

She endeavoured to keep the desperation from her voice. 'Please . . .'

His eyes seared hers, lancing right through to her soul. After what seemed an interminable silence, he drawled, 'Have dinner with me tonight.' He named a well-known restaurant. 'Meet me there. Seven-thirty.'

Her lips formed a single negation, only to have it remain locked in her throat.

'A test of filial loyalty, wouldn't you agree?' He moved with lithe ease towards the door. 'My secretary will see you out.'

*   *   *

A shiver shook Elise's slim frame as the image disappeared and, no matter how hard she concentrated, it was impossible to recall.

Alejandro paused beside her, his expression intent as his eyes raked her pale cheeks. 'What is it?'

She lifted a hand and smoothed a stray tendril of hair back behind her ear. Slowly she turned towards him, her eyes shadowed and pensive.

'I was in your office.' She drew in a deep breath, then relayed a description. She looked at him, puzzlement creasing her forehead. 'I was appealing to you to extend my father's company loan,' she explained shakily. 'You were angry,' she revealed slowly. 'We both were.'

She'd felt it, *breathed* it in those few brief minutes, a palpable entity so vivid it made her feel terribly afraid.

His expression was impossible to fathom. 'How much were you able to remember?'

Was that why she'd married Alejandro? To save her father?

Her head began to reel, and she drew a deep breath in a conscious effort to stave off a spell of dizziness.

'You were called in to a board meeting,' she revealed slowly, trying desperately to recall the elusive image without success. 'I can remember walking to the lift, stepping into it,' she said helplessly. 'But that's all.'

His hands lifted to cradle her face, then his mouth closed over hers in a light tasting that elicited little response. It was as if her mind were still caught up with the desire to recapture the past, and she didn't offer a word as they made their way back to the house.

Elise found it difficult to shake off an inclination towards introspection for the rest of the day, and even during dinner she was unusually quiet.

'Anxiety won't help hasten the return of your memory,' Alejandro advised as she pushed her plate aside.

She glimpsed the inherent strength apparent, and her eyes took on a shadowy quality. 'I can't help the feeling of defencelessness that has always lurked in the background,' she revealed slowly, holding his gaze.

'You have no reason to be uncertain. About anything,' he added with deliberate emphasis.

She wasn't quite so sure, but at the moment she had little option but to accept his word.

He rose to his feet and began collecting cutlery and stacking plates. 'Sort through the video cassettes while I take care of the dishes.'

Elise wandered into the informal lounge, and after some deliberation she selected an action movie that threatened to swamp the viewer with lots of thrills and spills.

Alejandro walked into the room just as the previews concluded, and as she made for one of the single chairs he tugged her down on to the two-seater beside him.

With maximum ease he adjusted their positions so that she rested between his thighs and leaned back against his chest. His hands moved to link together over her lower abdomen.

The desire to stay there overcame any willingness to protest, and she forced herself to concentrate on the superbly fit male actor on screen as he launched into a daring choreographic karate routine with his opponent.

Elise must have fallen into a doze at some stage, for when she woke she was in bed and it was morning.

After a leisurely breakfast Alejandro tossed their bags into the boot, locked up the house, and drove back to the city.

'You look so much better,' Ana beamed with approval as she greeted them on arrival, and her pleasant features creased into a genuine smile. 'It is good to see the colour in your face again.'

Elise's mouth curved with a certain wry humour. 'Alejandro has been feeding me up and taking me for walks along the beach.'

'I will serve lunch early. Your appointment is at two, *si*?'

It was all going to start: the daily physiotherapy sessions, the visits to specialists, and soon there would be no reason for her not to rejoin Alejandro on the social scene.

Elise was unable to still a feeling of instinctive apprehension, and although she did justice to a bowl of Ana's chicken soup, she toyed with the salad, picked at the bread, and opted to conclude the meal with fresh fruit.

Perhaps José would drive her to the physio-therapist's rooms, leaving Alejandro to retire into the study for the rest of the afternoon.

However, it was her inimitable husband who slid in behind the wheel.

'There's no need for you to come in with me,' she essayed when the Bentley eased into a parking bay adjacent to the main entrance.

'I'll confine myself to the waiting-room,' Alejandro conceded with amused tolerance, and she wrinkled her nose at him in silent admonition as he followed her in to reception.

The physiotherapist explained precisely what exercises he wanted her to do, and why—muscles lost their elasticity if they were not used, resulting in stiffness, gradual loss of mobility, and pain.

Elise completed the simple exercises with supervised care, and at the end of the session Alejandro drove her home.

Traffic was congested, some drivers more impatient than others as the lines of cars slowed to a snail's pace. Tempers rose, horns blared and engines roared in protest. Then slowly they began to move again.

The Bentley had just begun to pick up speed when Alejandro hit the brakes. Elise was conscious of several things at once: Alejandro's arm anchoring her against the seat an instant before the car lurched on impact, and the sickening sound of crunching metal. She registered dimly a string of viciously articulated Spanish words, then Alejandro was leaning over her, his features harsh as his hands cupped her face.

'Are you all right?'

She was in another car, a white sports model, behind the wheel, passing through a computer-controlled intersection. There was an instantaneous reaction as she slammed on the brakes and wrenched the wheel in a desperate bid to avoid hitting the oncoming vehicle. But it was too late. There was a sickening crunch of metal. Her head hit something, and then there was darkness.

'*Por Dios*.'

Elise felt as if her eyes were far too large for her face as she attempted to re-focus them and shut out that horrific vision.

'Are you hurt?'

She registered Alejandro's voice, deep, dark and throbbing, then she saw his face, anxiety etching every line, his eyes almost black as they attempted to see beyond the mask her features had become.

'Elise.' His fingers were gentle as they stroked each cheek, and she blinked once, twice, then she was back in the present.

'I'm—fine,' she attempted, through lips that trembled badly. She met his intent gaze, and swallowed the sudden lump that seemed lodged in her throat. 'Really,' she assured him shakily as she defended herself against eyes that seemed to pierce her soul.

'You remembered the accident.' It was a statement, not a query. 'All of it?'

Her lips seemed strangely dry, and she edged out the tip of her tongue to moisten them. 'Just—a blur of blue hurtling towards me, the moment of impact.'

His eyes never left her face, and her mouth trembled slightly as he reached for the car-phone, punched in a series of numbers, requested the police, and gave a brief description of the accident and location.

Elise could only stare straight ahead as Alejandro pushed open the door and slid to his feet, and his hard inflexible tones combining with those of the man who had tempted providence by making an erroneous move barely penetrated her conscious mind.

Was this how her memory would return? A series of brief isolated incidents every few days?

Seconds later Alejandro slid in behind the wheel, and Elise bore his intent scrutiny with equanimity.

'I'm OK,' she assured him. 'Is there much damage to the car?'

'*You* concern me. Not the car,' he said bleakly.

At some stage she heard the distant wail of a police siren, then it came close, red and blue lights flashing. Doors slammed, voices.

It wasn't until they arrived home that she saw the broken light and its surround, the deep gouges and scratches. The sight of them brought on a wave of nausea, and she only just made it upstairs in time.

No protest she made prevented Alejandro from calling in the doctor.

'Dammit, this is *normal*,' she uttered fiercely, and saw his expression measurably harden. She lifted her hands in mock surrender. 'All right, I give in.'

An hour later she barely refrained from reiterating the doctor's reassurance, and the only concession she made to resting was to recline on the sun-lounger beneath a shade umbrella at the pool's edge.

The next few days assumed a regular routine as Elise attended the physiotherapy clinic and kept an appointment with the neurologist.

Alejandro rose early, spent an hour working out in the downstairs gym, followed it with several lengths in the pool, then after breakfast he closeted himself in the study until Ana served lunch.

An urgent telephone call on Friday morning necessitated his presence in the city, and Elise rejoiced at the thought of spending the day alone.

The physiotherapy session was scheduled for mid-morning, and after lunch she settled down to leaf through a supply of the latest glossy magazines.

Tall, perfectly proportioned young women modelling beautiful clothes, she perceived as she flipped idly through the fashion pages.

One model in particular caught her eye, and she wondered at her instinctive fascination with a long-haired brunette with classical features and cool dark eyes.

Without any warning those same features seemed to come alive, and it was like watching a re-run of part of a film depicting an isolated incident in her life, Elise decided, momentarily freezing as images crowded her brain. So clear, so hauntingly vivid.

Alejandro, Elise and Savannah seated together at a table, aiding one of several charities Alejandro was known to support.

Savannah. The hauntingly beautiful model who had been Alejandro's close companion for several years before Elise had been thrust into the limelight as his latest conquest.

Now Savannah seemed intent on proving she still held Alejandro's interest by indulging in a little game of subtle flirting, a fact which was not lost on Elise.

It was extremely difficult to maintain the semblance of a smile as she spooned morsels of delectable fruit from the elaborately presented dessert.

Jealousy was a terrible emotion, she conceded, as she picked up her fork and speared a segment of orange with more force than necessary. With little provocation, she could have killed Savannah for her blatant attempt to capture Alejandro's attention. As for Alejandro... She would have liked to do temporary harm to a vulnerable part of his anatomy.

Perhaps he sensed her antipathy, for he turned his head and his eyes gleamed with mild amusement as he met her calculated smile.

Without a word he reached for her hand and carried it to his lips, kissing each finger in turn as she seethed with silent anger.

How dared he? She wanted to walk out and take a taxi home. As it was, she barely managed to preserve a calm front for the remainder of the evening, and the instant Alejandro brought the Bentley to a halt inside the garage she burst into angry speech.

'In future you can choose whether you partner Savannah or your wife,' Elise railed in fury.

'You expect me to display ill manners by ignoring a friend I have known for several years?'

'Heaven forbid,' Elise said sarcastically.

'You have no reason to be jealous.'

She slid from the car as he moved out from behind the wheel, and it gave her the utmost satisfaction to slam the door.

'I am not jealous. I simply refuse to be part of a *ménage-à-trois*.'

Alejandro began to chuckle, and the husky sounds of his amusement acted like flame placed too close to combustible octane.

Elise threw her evening bag at him, and followed it with one evening sandal, then the other, each of which he neatly fielded and slid into the pockets of his jacket.

'So you want to play?'

He reached her far too easily, before she had gone more than a few steps, and she gasped in outrage as he lifted her effortlessly over one shoulder and carried her indoors.

'Put me down!'

He walked through the foyer to the stairs, gaining the upper floor with galling ease, seemingly uncaring as she beat her hands against the broad expanse of his back.

In the bedroom he tumbled her down on to the bed, discarded his jacket, then captured her wildly scrambling form by the simple expedient of covering it with his own.

'Damn you,' Elise vented as she struggled impotently against his superior strength. 'I hate you.'

'I love the way you hate, *mi mujer*.'

'Sex. Lust,' she qualified. 'Bought and paid for.'

He went curiously still. 'I suggest you retract that vilifying statement.'

'Why? Does the truth penetrate your conscience, Alejandro?' she taunted, only to cry out in shocked surprise as his mouth closed over hers with punishing force.

What followed was a form of retribution he actively encouraged her to share, their mingling anger resulting in wild, untamed sex that gave no quarter... for either of them.

'Elise?'

The sound of Ana's voice seemed to come from far away, and Elise dragged her mind back to the present. Her heart pounded inside her chest, and her skin was damp with the fine sheen of sweat.

'I have just made tea. Would you like some?'

Somehow she managed a suitable response.

Dear God. This was the most explicit span she'd experienced. The memory of it was so vivid, the act so primitively savage that it was all she could do to prevent herself from being physically ill.

I don't want to remember any more. Not if total recall means a revival of anger and dissension.

The friendship, the special closeness which she and Alejandro had shared at Palm Beach seemed part of a distant fantasy.

Instinct warned her that she was teetering on the edge of reality, and a chill feathered over her skin, raising all her fine body-hairs in protective defence.

CHAPTER SIX

IT RAINED most of the weekend, squally wind-driven showers that beat against the windows, bringing much-needed water to the city's depleted dams and providing relief against the seasonal threat of bushfires.

Alejandro taught Elise the basic skills of chess, checkmating her so many times that she declined to allow him further victory as she opted to trounce him at cards. That too was a disaster, for, although she won twice, she suspected that it was only because he deliberately set out to lose.

Monday dawned bright and clear. The Bentley went in for repair, and Alejandro took the Porsche into the city.

Elise attended physiotherapy after lunch, then José drove her across town for her appointment with the obstetrician. They arrived early, and she opted to check in rather than wait in the car.

The senior nurse greeted her warmly. 'Doctor has a patient with him, Mrs Santanas. He won't be long.' Elise took a seat, selected a magazine, and began leafing through the pages. An article caught her eye, and she read it with interest.

Minutes later she glanced absently at another, and froze. Two frames featuring Savannah adorned facing pages, and with a tiny gasp of shock everything suddenly fell into place, almost as if someone had depressed a camera shutter, then released it to reveal a moving photograph to view.

With horrified fascination she watched it all unfold.

Dear heaven, no. *No.* The negation seemed to thunder inside her brain over and over as she desperately sought to stop the images appearing one after the other like a rolling reel of Technicolor film.

It wasn't true. None of it. There was some terrible mistake. A shocking joke played by a devilish hand.

If she sat still, perfectly still, the images would disappear, and she could walk out of here without becoming an emotional wreck.

Her stomach churned as the impact of recurring memory took effect, and she only just made it to the powder-room in time.

Afterwards, she leaned her head against the cool tiles for several minutes as she stared sightlessly at the beautifully appointed bathroom.

She didn't feel like facing anyone, much less a skilfully perceptive medical professional who would doubtless take one look at her pale features, note her elevated pulse-rate, and begin a line of questioning she had no wish to answer.

Elise wondered what sort of reaction she would generate if she simply walked out, slid into the waiting car, and bade José take her home.

Home. Hell's teeth, how could she go *there*? How could she not? she decided dully. If she requested José to take her anywhere else, it would only be a matter of minutes before José alerted Alejandro, and then what? A confrontation?

She had so much anger to expel. Such a degree of inner rage.

With deplorable ease her mind slid back to the ill-fated dinner she had shared with Alejandro Santanas only hours after launching a personal appeal for him to stave off her father's imminent fall into bankruptcy...

Elise arrived five minutes late and was escorted to Alejandro's table where, within minutes of ordering iced water, she immediately launched a further attempt on Joseph Hansen's behalf.

'What inducement do you intend to offer me?' He lifted one well-shaped eyebrow, his expression assuming world-weary cynicism. 'Yourself, perhaps?'

It took mere seconds for his words to sink in, a few more for her to throw the contents of her glass at his face. She rose to her feet in white-faced fury, then stormed from the restaurant...only to have to return when she discovered that she had left her evening bag on the table.

When she reached for it, his hand closed over hers.

'Sit down.'

'I have nothing to say to you!'

'Walk out on me a second time, and any chance you might have will be gone.'

Every instinct screamed for her to turn away from him, and it was only the image of her father that persuaded her to resume her seat.

'You care for your father very much.'

'If I didn't,' she responded flatly, 'I wouldn't be here.'

'Enough to give your personal guarantee to investment from my private funds?' His pause was deliberate. 'Become part of the deal?'

She felt cold, and barely in control. 'In what capacity?' If he said as his mistress, she would tip the soup in his lap, then walk away. This time she would make sure she had her bag. And hell would freeze over before she would willingly exchange so much as a word with him should their paths meet again.

'My wife.'

It was the last thing she had expected him to say. 'You're insane.'

He subjected her to a long, steady look before venturing in a hateful drawl, 'Two million dollars as an unconditional gift in exchange for two years of your life.'

'No.'

'You sign a pre-nuptial agreement relinquishing any claim on my assets in lieu of the two million dollars I advance to your father on the day of our marriage,' he continued as if she hadn't spoken.

It was totally crazy. 'No.'

'Handsome recompense for an act of mercy.'

'My father would never condone it.'

'He need not know, if you act a part.' His eyes never left hers. 'You have twenty-four hours to reach a decision.'

She gave it, within mere minutes of his deadline.

The marriage of Elise Hansen and Alejandro Santanas took place a week later.

'If it were not for my father,' Elise vented with restrained vehemence as she attached her signature to the marriage register, 'I would never have agreed to this diabolical arrangement.'

'I have no doubt.'

'What if I refuse you?' she flung at him later that night when they retired to their hotel suite.

'A no I should interpret as a maybe?' Alejandro queried. 'If my foreplay succeeds in arousing you to a state of sensual desire?'

'You damned egotist,' she spluttered.

Afterwards she hated herself, *him*, for proving that sex and love were two entirely different emotions.

It had taken only weeks to discover the existence of Savannah and learn that the glamorous model had been and, rumour had it, still was Alejandro's mistress—a revelation deliberately designed to shatter her confidence. At the time, the vindictive gossip did not hurt at all. The pain came later.

Four months after her marriage her father suffered a heart attack, partly recovered, only to incur a second massive attack in a matter of weeks.

The night he lay so ill in hospital after the initial attack she forgot to take the Pill. By the time she realised the implications of her lapse it was too late, and her worst fears were confirmed when a home pregnancy test showed positive. A doctor's appointment merely verified it.

For two weeks she suffered the tortures of the damned. Then, early one morning, soon after Alejandro left for the office, she simply threw a few clothes into a bag, slid in behind the wheel of the Porsche Carrera and headed north.

Ironically, she had only cleared the outer suburbs when another car ran through a 'Stop' sign.

She could vividly recall her reaction as she slammed on the brakes and made a desperate effort to avoid him; the sickening sound of colliding metal; a shuddering jolt that threw her against the door. Then nothing.

Elise's head was throbbing so badly that at first she didn't hear the repeated knock at the door.

'Mrs Santanas? Are you all right?'

Oh, God. How long had she been in here? Five minutes . . . ten?

'Yes. An attack of nausea,' she reassured the nurse shakily. She'd have to pull herself together. She looked and felt like death. 'I'll be out in a minute.'

'Doctor is ready to see you. Can I get you a cool drink? A cup of tea?'

There were disposable toothbrushes and toothpaste thoughtfully provided, and she made use of both before applying lipstick and running a comb through her hair. 'Tea would be lovely. Thanks.'

Ten minutes later she sat in a deep cushioned chair facing a small middle-aged man, who viewed her over half-moon spectacles resting halfway down the bridge of his nose.

'You're pale, and your pulse-rate is elevated,' he declared quietly. 'Care to tell me what's bothering you?'

'The baby——'

'Is fine. The mother, however, is giving me cause for concern.' He subjected her to a lengthy appraisal, then ventured gently, 'Your memory. Have you experienced any recurring flashes?'

She wanted to deny them, for, if she pretended they hadn't occurred, she might somehow fool herself they were part of some horrid nightmare that had no place in reality.

'A few,' she admitted cautiously, unwilling to relay that her memory had returned in full.

'You've found them distressing?'

Partial truth was infinitely preferable to truth in its entirety. 'I guess it's a natural reaction. My husband has been able to fill in some details, but not all.'

'I think I should call him.'

'*No*. No,' she hastened quickly, aware of his sharp interest. 'Please.'

He looked thoughtful. 'He has been very concerned about you.' He didn't add that Alejandro Santanas had insisted on a full report after every one of his wife's consultations. 'I think it would be best if I see you again in a fortnight. Finish your tea.'

José was waiting in the car when she emerged, and as soon as he caught sight of her he moved quickly round to open the rear door, then, when she was safely seated, he slid in behind the wheel.

'Is there anywhere you would like to go? A little shopping, perhaps?'

She had money, and sufficient credit-card buying power to walk into any store and purchase literally anything. For a moment she was tempted to indulge in a splurge that would raise her husband's eyebrows when he received the bill. But she had an entire closet full of fashionable clothes, enough shoes to wear a different pair every day for a number of weeks. Perfume, toiletries, make-up. Even jewellery. Alejandro had been exceedingly generous, given the circumstances of their marriage. She related such generosity to the need to project the image of a successful man's wife.

'Double Bay, José,' she instructed on a sudden whim. 'Alejandro is entertaining a business associate tonight, and I have an inclination to buy a new outfit.'

'*Sí*,' José concurred with a friendly grin. 'I shall take you there.'

The car slid forward, moving out into the flow of traffic, and Elise leaned back against the cushioned seat and closed her eyes against the onset of images crowding her brain.

'Would you like me to accompany you?'

Elise blinked at the sound of José's voice, and hastily caught hold of her scattered thoughts as she established that the Bentley was parked outside one of several exclusive boutiques known for their designer labels and expensive price-tags.

'No, thank you, José.' She cast him a warm smile. 'Why don't you have coffee somewhere? I'll be at least half an hour.'

She was twice that time and more, requiring special authorisation when it became apparent that she was unable to sign the appropriate credit slips.

They arrived home only minutes ahead of Alejandro, and she moved quickly upstairs to their suite in the hope of avoiding him...at least momentarily. If she hurried, she might be able to seclude herself in the shower.

She managed it, but only just, and when she emerged into the bedroom he was in the process of discarding his clothes.

Her eyes encountered his, then skittered away as he pulled off his shirt and took the few necessary steps to reach her.

For a few more hours at least, she had to act a part. After their dinner guests departed, she could unleash her inner rage.

The need to say something—anything—seemed paramount, and she rushed into speech. 'José took me to Double Bay. Shopping,' she elaborated, indicating the assortment of brightly coloured carrier bags at the foot of the bed. 'I felt like wearing something new tonight.' He was within touching distance, and she injected warmth into her smile as he lifted both hands to cup her face.

His mouth closed over hers, warm, hungry, possessive. She could feel her own unbidden response, the unfurling deep within as he drew her close in against him.

When he lifted his head it was all she could do to meet the dark intentness of his gaze, and she felt her lips tremble as he gently rubbed his thumb back and forth across the kiss-swollen curves.

One hand traced a path down her neck to trail the edge of her silk robe, parting it to slip inside and caress the full curve of her breast. 'What did the obstetrician have to say?'

How did she answer that? With extreme care, a tiny voice warned. 'He reassured me that the baby is fine.'

Her breasts felt heavy, their peaks taut and aching. It wasn't the only part of her that ached. *Dammit*, how could her body react in such a traitorous fashion?

His eyes seared hers, dark and analytical, almost as if he knew precisely what had happened and was waiting for her to tell him.

Could the obstetrician have called him? The possibility wouldn't surprise her. 'I—suffered a bout of morning sickness.' She paused, then made a light attempt at humour. 'In the middle of the afternoon.' She was not such a good actress that Alejandro would be fooled for long. 'I had another memory flash.' It was an extension of the truth. 'It shook me up a little.'

'Poor *niña*,' Alejandro soothed, brushing his lips against her temple. 'If you don't feel up to dinner tonight, I will contact André and have him meet me at a restaurant.'

'No,' Elise said quickly, adding, 'Ana has gone to a lot of trouble.' She didn't want to wake in the depths of night when he slid into bed and reached for her.

She wanted a confrontation. Dammit, she wanted to launch a full-scale war against him. But not when they had a guest due to arrive for dinner in—how long? Less than an hour?

'Shouldn't we get ready?'

Alejandro drew back and gave her a rueful smile. 'I need to shower and shave.'

The dress she had bought was a slim-fitting sheath in a brilliant red uncrushable viscose and linen mix, its hemline resting just above the knee. A clever panel of red beaded embroidery elevated the simple design to the glamorous, and matching beaded shoes completed an ensemble that shrieked a top Australian label.

Alejandro entered the bedroom as she put the finishing touches to her make-up, and with practised ease he attended to the hook on her bra, then assisted her into the dress. The long zip-fastener slid home, and she slowly turned to face him.

'Stunning,' he pronounced, his eyes gleaming with indolent appreciation as they roved over her slim curves. 'Do you need help with your hair?'

'I thought I'd wear it loose.'

She crossed to the dressing-table and caught up her brush, stroking the length of her hair until it shone. Ear-rings were too difficult to attach with one hand, so she discarded the idea.

André Valery was a tall, handsome man in his late thirties, charming, with Gallic appreciation for the opposite sex.

'I have been looking forward to meeting the woman who managed to slip beneath Alejandro's armour.' He lifted his glass in salute. 'I congratulate you.'

Dinner was a success, for not only had Ana excelled herself with superb culinary offerings, but the delicate baiting each man indulged in bore the stamp of a long friendship.

'You realise our fathers were business associates? *Oui*. It is true. For some years we spent holidays together. Gstaad. St Moritz. One year Alejandro was packed off to join my family in Paris.' His eyes twinkled with wicked humour. 'We were young, gregarious, and, I think, a little too adventurous for our own good.'

'Don't indulge in tales, André,' Alejandro drawled, 'or I may feel compelled to relay a few of my own to Anne-Marie when next I see her.'

'Anne-Marie,' André returned, with a Gallic shrug, 'is in no doubt as to what manner of man I am.'

'Are you about to destroy my illusions?' Elise queried lightly, and incurred his slight smile. His eyes, however, assumed inscrutability.

'What illusions do you refer to, *chérie*?'

'That you might be an exception to most successful men and have chosen not to have both wife and mistress?'

André's gaze didn't waver, and she met it fearlessly, aware of the sudden stillness in the room. 'If a man values his family, and his wife meets his needs,' he offered quite gently, 'why would there be the necessity for him to take a mistress?'

She was stepping into dangerous territory, but she didn't care. 'The challenge it represents, perhaps? Excitement?' She managed a careless shrug. 'Would you consider it fair for a wife to expect her needs also to be met?'

Alejandro's voice was pure silk. 'You are lodging a subtle complaint, *querida*?'

It took all her acting ability, but she managed a light incredulous laugh. 'How could I begin to fault you?' She reached out a placating hand, and sat quite still as he took hold of it and raised her fingers to his lips.

It was a deliberate gesture, and she glimpsed the dark gleam in his eyes, a watchfulness that sent warning flares licking the taut edge of her nerves.

He knew. Perhaps not precisely *when* her memory had returned, but there was no doubt he was aware that she had experienced a total recall.

'Shall we adjourn to the lounge for coffee?' Alejandro suggested smoothly.

Somehow Elise managed to get through the rest of the evening. If André sensed that her conversation was a little too bright, he gave no indication.

'You must excuse me,' André said at last. 'It is late, and I must return to my hotel.' He crossed to her side. 'Thank you for a most enjoyable evening.' He took her hand and lifted it to his lips, then held it a fraction longer than was necessary. 'Alejandro must bring you to Paris,' he said gently. 'It would give Anne-Marie much pleasure.'

'Indeed,' Alejandro concurred as they moved through to the front of the house.

Elise turned away from the door the instant the car's tail-lights cleared the gates, acutely conscious of Alejandro's actions as he re-set the alarm system.

Apprehension prickled at the back of her neck as she made for the stairs. The anger that had lain dormant since this afternoon rose to the fore, darkening her eyes and reining her mouth into a firm line.

Entering the bedroom, she slipped off her shoes, then reached for the zip-fastening at the back of her dress.

Alejandro came into the room as she began a third fruitless attempt to slide the fastener down, and she didn't utter a word as he crossed to complete the task.

With extreme care she stepped out of the dress and placed it over a nearby chair, watching out of the corner of her eye as he discarded his jacket and removed his tie.

'When did it happen?'

His voice was quiet, deadly, and she turned slowly to face him, unwilling to prevaricate.

Eyes as dark as onyx were filled with a chilling intensity, and her chin tilted fractionally as she prepared to oppose him.

'This afternoon. In the obstetrician's waiting-room.' Her eyes sparked with green fire. 'A photograph of Savannah in a magazine acted as the trigger, giving me total recollection in slow motion.'

His expression darkened fractionally, and he reached out a hand, catching hold of her chin between thumb and forefinger, tightening his grasp when she attempted to wrench it away.

Elise's eyes flared a brilliant topaz-flecked emerald in unspoken challenge. '*Why?*' she demanded. 'Why did you deceive me?'

He held her effortlessly, his expression an inscrutable mask. His silence angered her immeasurably.

'Dammit, *answer* me!'

His eyes became bleak, and his voice sounded as dark as the depths of his black soul. '*When* would you have had me reveal facts?'

She suffered his raking scrutiny with angry defiance as she waited for him to continue.

'While you lay in a hospital bed injured and afraid?' he pursued relentlessly. 'When you first came home?' His eyes dared her to refute him. 'Should I have destroyed your trust? Refused you reassurance and affection?'

'You took advantage with a calculated play on my emotions,' she cried, raw with pain.

'We made love,' Alejandro corrected harshly.

'We had *sex*.'

'A carnal coupling?' His voice was lethal. 'Based on greed and the gratification of a primitive urge?'

Dear God, it hadn't been like that. Ever. No matter how hard she fought, she had been entrapped from the moment of confrontation in his office. One look, and she'd been shaken to the very roots of her being by the mesmeric quality of his masculinity. Aware, with the depth of self-knowledge, that Alejandro Santanas possessed the ability to render her helpless as no other man could. She had hated him for it, hated herself for her own vulnerability. But, most of all, she had hated the circumstances that bound her to him.

She wanted to cry out a rejection, but the words choked in her throat. 'The night of the accident,' she revealed bleakly, 'I'd decided to leave you.'

His eyes speared her. 'How long did you imagine it would take before I tracked you down?'

'I intended to see a lawyer and file for separation.'

His features hardened measurably. 'You hate me so much that you would attempt to deny me knowledge of your pregnancy, my child's existence?' His voice lowered to a dangerous silkiness that sent tiny shivers along her spine. 'Or did you plan an abortion?'

'*No*,' she jerked out in shocked denial, reasserting in a hushed tone, 'No.' The thought had never entered her head.

He was silent for several interminable minutes, and when he spoke his voice was hard and held unaccountable bleakness. 'The child you carry is as much mine as yours. Uniquely *ours*. Our son or daughter deserves to be more than someone we fight custody for in a law court.'

'I married you because I couldn't stand by and see my father emotionally and financially beaten. It would have killed him.' She had to take some consolation from the knowledge that the last few months of his life had been happy. 'You engineered a diabolical game,' she accused him fiercely. 'I should have damned you to the depths of hell and walked away.'

He regarded her steadily for what seemed an age. 'Yet you didn't,' he reminded her, his gaze alert beneath partly lowered lids. 'You accepted the arrangement as a challenge, and attempted to score against me.'

That had been her intention. At first, she had fooled herself that she was succeeding. Except that somewhere along the way she had fallen in love with him.

'Displaying beautiful manners in public,' he went on in musing reflection, 'while behaving like a virago when we were alone.'

Her eyes were dark and accusing. 'A fact you deliberately withheld from me.'

'If you remember,' Alejandro pursued, 'I made no pretence that we shared an idyllic relationship.'

'You said we argued occasionally!' Elise flung, hating his skilful employment of words.

'Frequently,' he corrected. 'The resolving of such arguments was always——' he paused deliberately '—satisfactory, wouldn't you say?'

That was an understatement. In bed, they had always been in perfect accord. In the beginning it had been a source of anguish, for she found it difficult to condone the degree of her emotional involvement with a man she professed to hate.

'Our marriage breaks all the rules,' she offered wretchedly, her eyes stormy with anger, and her hand shook as she lifted it to push hair back from her face.

'The reason for its existence remains the same,' he said in a hard voice.

She looked at him carefully, aware of his immense strength of will, the arresting elemental quality that made her feel suddenly afraid. 'You can't mean for the marriage to continue?'

'Indeed,' Alejandro declared inflexibly. He subjected her to a long, level appraisal. 'What is more, I insist that you honour the two-year term listed in our pre-nuptial agreement.'

Anger emanated from every pore in her body. 'That's barbaric!'

'Perhaps.' His smile was a mere facsimile, his eyes dark and forbidding.

'You expect me to act a part?' She felt like screaming with indignant resentment. '*Pretend*?'

His expression was resolute, and his voice held infinite mockery. 'You have managed admirably for the past seven months.'

'*Six*,' she flung back angrily, incensed by his imperturbability. 'I cannot be held responsible for the past one and a half.'

He lifted a hand and brushed light fingers along the edge of her jaw. 'Relieved of the barriers of your animosity for a few short weeks,' he said, 'there was no reason to generate hatred for your Spanish *esposo*.'

She closed her eyes, then slowly opened them again. 'There wasn't meant to be a child!' It was a cry from the heart.

His voice gentled as he caught hold of her chin and tilted it towards him. 'Nevertheless, there is. Its unexpected existence is something I refuse to consider as anything other than a very special gift.' His thumb lightly caressed the lower edge of her lip. 'For several weeks we were able to dispense with any hostility.' His eyes darkened measurably. 'Friends, as well as lovers.'

Her eyes glittered with anger, sheer emerald flecked with gold. 'We can never be friends!'

A smile tinged with wry mockery tugged the edges of his mouth. 'Perhaps at this moment you do not believe so.' Dark eyes gleamed with cynical humour. 'Why don't you get into bed?'

Her pulse tripped its beat and measurably quickened—as a result of anger, she assured herself, not passion. 'I don't want to go to bed, and I especially don't want to share a bed with you.'

'We share, Elise,' he insisted in a dangerously soft voice, 'as we have done from the beginning.'

His threat wasn't an idle one, and she looked at him in silent mutiny for several long seconds. 'If you touch me, so help me, I'll *hit* you,' she vouched with low-pitched vehemence, and, turning away from him, she caught up her nightgown and crossed into the bathroom to remove her make-up.

Her fingers shook so badly that the cream got into her eyes, and she dabbed frantically at it before sluicing her face.

Alejandro was in bed when she emerged, stretched out, his arms crossed behind his head.

Elise eyed him warily as she slipped in beneath the covers and closed her eyes. Seconds later she heard the snap of the bedside lamp as the room was plunged into darkness.

Slowly her lashes swept upwards, and for a long time she stared sightlessly ahead, discerning shadows and a thin strip of moonlight threading between the curtains as her eyes adjusted to the grey light of night.

She was acutely aware of every sound, her own breathing, his, and she knew the moment when Alejandro's steadied and assumed a deep rhythmic beat.

Tomorrow, she promised as her eyelids became heavy and began to flutter down. Tomorrow she would launch an attack about the depth of his involvement with the glamorous Savannah.

CHAPTER SEVEN

ELISE woke late to discover that Alejandro had already left for the city. His absence provided an anticlimax, for there was a fine edge to her inner rage that longed for the satisfaction of a full-scale confrontation.

'Alejandro asked me to tell you that you are both to attend a formal dinner to aid charity this evening,' Ana conveyed as Elise sat down to a solitary breakfast.

The Santanas Corporation was a well-known benefactor, and Alejandro lent his personal patronage to selected organisations. Elise had attended several such dinners in the past, and her heart sank at the thought of mingling with Alejandro's sophisticated coterie of acquaintances.

Without doubt Savannah would be present, and Elise hated being an object of conjecture as certain guests speculated on the latest developments between the Santanas scion, his wife, and the glamorous model who had been his constant companion for years before his sudden marriage to a virtual unknown with no social background.

Elise entertained no doubt that Alejandro's absence from the social scene for the past six weeks had been duly noted and commented upon, details regarding her accident embellished and explicated.

It seemed coincidental that she was to have the bandages removed from her hand today. After this afternoon, physiotherapy would be reduced to weekly instead of daily sessions. Soon the only evidence would be a thin scar on her hand.

The thought of regaining her independence was a heady one. After today, she would be able to drive again. There were a few friends she needed to contact. *Siobhan*. Realisation suddenly hit her that her dearest friend might be anxious not to have heard from her at all in the past six weeks.

As it was, she had no idea whether Siobhan was still working days at the Royal Children's Hospital, or if she had crossed over to night duty. If it was nights, the answering machine would be on and she could leave a message.

Elise checked the time, then finished her breakfast and moved quickly upstairs to use the bedroom telephone.

Siobhan picked up on the third ring, her voice jubilant on discovering who was on the other end of the line, and they talked for the best part of an hour before Elise reluctantly had to conclude the call in order to keep her appointment with the orthopaedic surgeon.

'Let's meet for lunch— *soon*,' she insisted.

'I'm a working girl, remember?' Siobhan teased. 'However, I'm off the next two nights. Is tomorrow soon enough?'

Elise gave an exultant laugh. 'Tomorrow it is. Just name the place, the time, and I'll be there.'

An hour later José deposited her outside the consultant orthopaedist's rooms, and thirty minutes later she walked out *sans* protective half-cast and bandages. The specialist sanctioned a return to driving, advised care with her hand, and suggested a further appointment in a month.

Now all she had to do was determine which car she could use as her own. There had been no mention of the white Porsche or its fate. Surely it couldn't have been smashed beyond repair? With the Bentley out of action, Alejandro was taking the Porsche Targa into the city, which left the Pajero wagon for José. She would have to broach it with Alejandro tonight.

After lunch she went through the contents of her wardrobe in an effort to reach a decision over what to wear to dinner, and after much deliberation she narrowed the choice down to two, eventually selecting a stunning fitted gown in deep emerald. The colour matched her eyes, highlighted the creamy texture of her skin, and proved a vivid contrast to her blonde hair.

It was almost four when José delivered her home from physiotherapy, and at five she took a shower, washed her hair and had Ana curl fat rollers into its length before attending to her nails.

Alejandro entered the bedroom as she began applying make-up, and she met his studied appraisal with equanimity.

'How is your hand?' He moved towards her, and Elise felt an immediate awareness of his close proximity.

Without a word she displayed the pink scar. 'I'm sure you've already received the specialist's report.' She hadn't intended to sound quite so cynical.

His eyes narrowed fractionally. 'Yes.'

'You also know that I am able to drive again,' she offered, watching as his head lowered down to hers.

She averted her head so that his kiss landed on her cheek, and almost at once he caught hold of her chin, anchoring it as he covered her mouth with his own in an invasion that brought forth a muffled entreaty he chose to ignore.

When he finally lifted his head she silently damned him to the depths of perdition.

The desire to rage against him was paramount, and, drawing in a deep breath, she launched into attack. 'I'd like to become independent again, rather than have to drag José away every time I want to go out.'

Alejandro slipped the knot free on his tie and began unfastening the buttons on his shirt. 'That is part of his job.'

Her eyes assumed a brilliant hue as anger began to unfurl, and it took considerable effort to control her temper. 'Have you assigned him as my gaoler?'

'You're being fanciful.'

'Am I?'

He looked every inch the power broker... indomitable, lethal, inflexible. 'Are you intent on having an argument?'

She wanted to throw something at him and have it cause mild bodily harm. 'I find it difficult to condone almost everything you do where I am concerned.'

He pulled his shirt free and tossed it down on to the bed. '*Almost* everything, *querida*?' One eyebrow slanted in silent mockery. 'Should I take that to indicate there is some hope for me?'

'Don't be so damned facetious,' she condemned fiercely, seething with helpless indignation as she glimpsed his amusement.

'We need to leave in half an hour. Can this discussion wait?'

'Until when, Alejandro?' she taunted, holding his gaze without any difficulty at all. 'Next week, next *month*?'

'Tomorrow.'

It was a better concession than she had hoped for, and she viewed him steadily for several long seconds as her anger began to dissipate.

'Where is the dinner being held tonight?'

One eyebrow arched, and his mouth assumed a degree of cynicism. 'The Sheraton.'

Some devilish imp prompted her to ask, 'Will Savannah be there?'

'I imagine so. She likes to attend most of the events.'

'In order to see *you*.' It was nothing less than the truth.

'Savannah has many friends, most of whom are active on the social circuit,' he drawled, and his faintly mocking tones brought a resurgence of anger.

'I can't think why you didn't marry her.' Elise endeavoured not to sound bitter. 'She would have leapt at the chance!'

'Perhaps,' Alejandro conceded, watching the play of emotions across her expressive features. 'I chose not to ask her.'

'One can only wonder why.' Her eyes deepened in colour and became faintly reflective. 'She's beautiful, poised, and she comes from the right social background.' It was amazing that her voice sounded so calm.

His eyes gleamed with sardonic humour. 'Many women of my acquaintance fit that description.'

'Several of whom are wealthy in their own right,' she pursued, uncaring that she was treading dangerous ground. 'Poor Alejandro,' she added lightly. 'Were you afraid their prime motivation was an advantageous financial merger? Or, if their independent wealth was sufficient for that not to be a consideration, could there have been distaste that they were merely lusting after your body? Not to mention your——' she hesitated deliberately, then finished with considered delicacy '—impressive skill in the bedroom.'

'Only in the bedroom, *mi mujer*?' he mocked cynically. 'I retain a vivid recollection of several enjoyable... encounters, shall we say?' he suggested, slanting one eyebrow. 'When we shared the shower, the spa.' His eyes gleamed as soft pink coloured her cheeks. 'Shall I continue?'

'You've had plenty of practice, damn you!'

'You are jealous, *querida*, that any one of my former lovers might possibly have meant more to me than you do?'

Elise felt her eyes widen with shock. Was she so transparent? Could he be aware of how much she hated the thought of his splendidly muscular body engaged in the act of lovemaking with another woman...? *Women*, she corrected. Past and present.

'How could I be jealous,' she countered, with as much pride as she could muster, 'when you clearly defined the reason for our marriage, allocated a price-tag and specified a time-limit?'

'That bothers you?'

It bothered her like hell, but she was damned if she would admit to it. 'About as much as the fact that you've chosen to retain Savannah as your mistress.'

'The term *mistress* conveys a woman kept by a husband while still co-habiting with his wife.' His eyes were dark, and held latent anger. 'You imagine I would insult you in such a manner?'

I don't know. 'I'd appreciate it if you would at least keep the... *liaison* discreet.'

There was a perceptible pause, one in which it seemed that even a pin falling to the floor would result in cacophonous sound. 'Am I to understand that you give your sanction to such a relationship?'

No. The silent negation screamed inside her head. It took tremendous effort to effect a slight shrug. 'Would anything I say make a difference?'

He appeared to be marshalling his anger, confining it beneath a mantle of superb control. 'We have a dinner engagement,' he reminded her icily. 'I suggest you get changed.'

The thought of sitting through a formal dinner in the company of some of the city's social glitterati was more than she could bear. 'Forgive me, Alejandro,' she said with bitter cynicism, 'but I can't bring myself to play pretend tonight.' Her eyes sparkled with emerald brilliance. 'I'm sure you can come up with some valid excuse that will explain my absence.' A devilish imp prompted her to add, 'Savannah will be delighted.'

He looked at her for what seemed an age, his expression a compelling mask from which she inwardly shrank. 'You tempt me to the brink of violence,' he said in a voice that was so dangerously quiet it raised all her fine body-hairs in silent fear.

Without a further word he discarded his clothes and strode into the bathroom. He didn't slam the door, and she found that infinitely more disquieting than if he had resorted to an outward display of anger.

Ten minutes later he emerged, a towel hitched low over his hips, and she moved hastily to her feet as he began to dress.

'Ask Ana to prepare you something to eat.'

'It's her night off,' Elise managed in a stilted voice. 'I wouldn't dream of disturbing her.' She crossed to the door. 'I'm quite capable of fixing something myself.'

She didn't wait for Alejandro to respond, and on reaching ground level she made her way to the kitchen.

The refrigerator was well stocked, so too was the pantry. It was just a matter of making a decision. An omelette would suffice, with cheese, tomato, ham, mushrooms... Not that she felt in the least hungry. If anything, the thought of food made her ill.

She removed a skillet, assembled the ingredients on the bench-top, then chopped, sliced and diced with methodical stoicism.

Alejandro entered the kitchen as she turned the omelette on to a plate, and she willed her hands not to betray her as she turned down the gas.

His raking appraisal unsettled her more than any words he could have chosen to utter, and she turned away from him as she carried her plate to the wide servery bench, then returned to collect cutlery.

She sensed rather than heard him move, and seconds later she felt his hands close over her shoulders as he turned her towards him.

For one achingly long moment their eyes clashed, then his head lowered in seemingly slow motion, and a strangled cry of dissent lay imprisoned in her throat as his mouth closed over hers in a hard merciless kiss that tore at her defences and reached right down to the depths of her soul.

It became a ruthless invasion that bordered on violation, and when at last he lifted his head, she could only stand in shocked immobility. If he had wanted to punish her, he'd succeeded, she decided numbly.

She felt raw, her whole body consumed by an emotional pain so intense that it was almost a tangible entity. Her eyes began to ache, then glistened with tears she refused to allow to fall.

His features were harsh, and with a muttered imprecation he turned and strode from the kitchen.

Minutes later she heard the muted sound of a car engine start up, then its refined purr diminished as it reached the end of the driveway.

She hugged her arms together, and tried valiantly to maintain a measure of control.

How long she stood there she had no idea, for she had no sense of the passage of time as she attempted to rationalise the foolishness of pitching her strength against a man whose physical and emotional strength were infinitely superior to her own.

It was only the prosaic need for food that refocused her attention, and with determined resolve she collected cutlery and systematically divided the cold omelette into bite-sized portions, forking them automatically into her mouth.

When she had finished, she cleaned the skillet, rinsed the plate and cutlery, and placed them in the dishwasher.

The house seemed incredibly silent, the lounge much too large for her to sit in alone. Feeling thoroughly unsettled, she wandered into the informal *sala*, collected a magazine, and sank into one of the deep cushioned seats. The pages were not able to capture her interest, and she discarded the magazine, choosing instead to use the remote module to switch on the television. Surely there would be something she could become involved in, she thought with despair, as she clicked one channel after another.

Two half-hour comedy shows provided some light relief, but her appreciation of the humour portrayed was only superficial, and when they were over she roved between the channels in search of a movie that might prove interesting.

There was not much selection, and she crossed to the cabinet and browsed through the collection of videos, discarding all but one. It was a dark Gothic piece that had earned critical acclaim, but she found it too intense, and was quite pleased when the credits finally rolled.

Elise crossed back into the kitchen and filled a glass with ice from the freezer, then added orange juice and slowly sipped the contents.

What time would Alejandro come home? If he came home, a tiny voice taunted. Dammit, of course he would. He had never stayed out before, so why would he begin now?

Maybe because you virtually gave him *carte blanche* to spend time with Savannah, the same tiny voice reminded her with devilish glee.

A glance at her watch revealed it to be after ten, and with sudden decisiveness she finished the juice, then made for the stairs. She would have a shower, then go to bed.

Twenty minutes later she slid beneath the cool linen sheets, snapped off the light, and closed her eyes.

Sleep did not provide the release she craved, and half an hour later she gave a muttered groan and slid out of bed, choosing to curl up in a chair close to the curtain-draped window.

How did one reconcile the heaven of loving Alejandro Santanas, and the resultant hell of knowing he could never love her? Elise reflected as she gazed sightlessly round the darkened room.

Like a moth at a flame, she had been struck by the lightning of instant attraction, aware of the swift invasive pull of sheer physical desire, and engulfed by its powerful magnetism.

By day she had fought him, hating him for being able to hold her captive to her own desire, hating herself for being so easily entrapped by the dictates of her own flesh . . . By night she lost the fight and revelled in the magic of his touch.

Would it ever be any different between them? It had been, she reflected sadly. For six short weeks she had believed him to be a caring, loving husband. A man who had devoted all of his time to her, and shown her incredible *tendresse*.

Had it been real? Or merely an act? She would probably never know.

Oh, hell, she cursed, as her eyes filled and tears began to trickle down both cheeks. She hardly ever cried. Except when her father had died. Dammit, her hormones must be raging some sort of inner war with her emotional heart. To be this stricken with tears was crazy.

Futile, she amended, timeless minutes later when she appeared all cried out. The spent emotion made her sleepy, and she snuggled deeper into the chair and rested her head in the curve of one arm.

It was there Alejandro found her, and he stood for a long time looking down at the graceful arch of her slender neck illuminated by the bedside lamp, the softness of her hair as it clung to her neck, the slender curves beneath the simple white cotton nightgown. And the faint evidence of tears.

Slowly he discarded his clothes, then he crossed back to the chair and carefully lifted her into his arms.

Elise stirred, aware in the depths of her subconscious that something was different. Whereas the cushioned chair was softly padded, now there was the warmth of hard muscular flesh beneath her head. She was aware of a deep rhythmic heartbeat, and an arm curving her close against a long male body. Fingers traced a light transient pattern over her hair, and she felt the brush of lips against her temple.

A soft sigh emerged from her lips, and almost in reflex action her arm crept out to encircle his waist.

His mouth was beautifully chiselled, and she knew exactly how it felt against her own. Even thinking about it brought alive the flicker of desire, igniting from her central core and licking treacherously along every nerve in her body.

Of its own accord her head angled slightly, the soft curves of her mouth parting to accept a kiss that began with incredible gentleness. Teasing, provocative, and profoundly seductive.

There was no thought of denying him, or herself, and she exulted in each caress, the overwhelming bewitching rapture as he guided her towards fulfilment—seismic, earth-shattering, a surrender to the sensual delights of passion.

It was the one level on which they communicated. No discord, no sense of disappointment. Just beautiful intimacy. Sex, she corrected, all too aware of the difference.

'Drop me anywhere along Oxford Street, José,' Elise declared. 'It's a beautiful day, and I feel like walking.'

The Pajero eased through the traffic-lights and pulled into a parking bay. 'What time, and where shall I collect you?'

'I'll get a taxi back,' she said lightly, unwilling to put a curfew on the day. Who knew how long lunch with Siobhan would extend? And besides, she might want to explore the shops for a while.

'Perhaps you will ring when you are ready?' José suggested on an anxious note. 'Alejandro would insist.'

Alejandro could insist all he liked! 'I'll let you know,' she conceded, feeling only slightly guilty that she had no intention of calling José. She proffered a warm smile, then opened the door and stepped down on to the pavement, waiting only a few seconds after he pulled out into the traffic before making her way towards the next street.

Siobhan was waiting for her, and they hugged each other as if it was years instead of several weeks since they had last seen each other.

'You look fantastic,' Siobhan declared as they entered the restaurant. The maître d' took them to a table with views of the harbour, handed them each a menu, then left them to make a selection. 'How is your hand?'

They ordered mineral water, deliberated over what they would eat, ordered, then attempted to continue where they had left off the previous afternoon.

Three hours later they shared the bill and wandered out into the fresh afternoon sunshine.

'The shops?' Siobhan hazarded with an irrepressible grin, laughing as Elise concurred with alacrity.

It was after five when they parted, promising to phone to arrange another lunch together the following week.

Taxis were in high demand, and the queue at the nearest rank was a lengthy one. Securing a taxi within half an hour looked to be impossible.

Damn, Elise cursed, aware that she should have taken the peak hour into consideration. Maybe a rank in one of the neighbouring streets would offer her a better opportunity.

It didn't. If anything, it was even longer. There wasn't much choice except to ring José.

She reached into her bag, then made a wry grimace on discovering that she had left the compact mobile phone at home. Locating a telephone booth took several minutes, and she had to wait for two people in front of her to take their turn in making calls.

Finally she got through, and the signal only sounded twice before the receiver was lifted from the hook. However, it wasn't José, or even Ana, who answered, and her heart took on an agitated beat.

'Where are you?'

Alejandro sounded so coldly furious that it was all she could do not to snap back at him.

'Downtown city. All the taxi ranks have horrendous queues.'

He appeared to be summoning control, and his anger emanated down the line. '*Where*, precisely, Elise?'

'Tell José I'll wait in Elizabeth Street, the Park Street end.'

However, it was the black Porsche which pulled into the kerb some thirty minutes later, not the Pajero.

One glance at Alejandro's harsh features was enough to determine that a battle was about to commence.

Alejandro leaned across and opened the passenger door. 'Get in.' His voice sounded clipped, and Elise slid in beside him and fastened her seatbelt.

It took the next change of lights before he could ease the Porsche ahead of the traffic, and their progress was hampered by the sheer number of vehicles vacating the city.

'I planned on being home before now.' It was a statement, not an apology.

'Obviously.'

Anger rose to the surface as she turned towards him. 'Dammit, Alejandro, I won't allow you to put me in a gilded cage!'

Something flickered in the depth of his eyes. 'My position in the business arena is well-reported in the Press.' A muscle tensed at the edge of his jaw. 'In today's society there are a few fanatics who take pleasure in targeting those who lead a high-profile existence. Consequently, I take extreme care to ensure any possible risks are kept to a minimum.' He spared her a dark glance, then returned his attention to negotiating the traffic. 'Hence the necessity for security measures. The reason I insist you always carry a mobile phone, and each vehicle has a car phone. A need for someone—myself, Ana, José—to be aware of your whereabouts. For protection. Not restriction.'

She lifted a hand in angry agitation. 'If I'd had my own car, this wouldn't have happened.'

He didn't say anything. He had no need, Elise decided darkly as the car cleared the city confines and traversed Bayswater Road. The traffic thinned slightly as they reached Double Bay, and ten minutes later the Porsche swung through the wide double gates at the entrance to the Point Piper mansion.

The garage doors lifted at a touch from Alejandro's remote module, then the car slid into place between the Pajero and a stunning red top-of-the-range Mercedes sedan.

'Yours,' Alejandro told her as she cast it an admiring glance.

Her stomach executed a slow flip, and she turned slowly towards him. 'You bought it for me?'

His expression was unfathomable. 'José will take you for a test-drive tomorrow.' He unclipped his belt and slid out from behind the wheel.

Elise did likewise, pausing long enough to run tentative fingers over the red satin-smooth paintwork. 'It's beautiful,' she said quietly and, taking a step towards him, she reached up and placed a fleeting kiss on the edge of his chin. 'Thank you.'

His mouth curved to form a wry smile, and his eyes assumed a darkness she found impossible to fathom.

'Your hand,' Alejandro asked quietly. 'How does it feel now the bandages and plaster have been removed?'

'A little strange. Stiff,' she elaborated with a slight shrug. 'Physiotherapy helps.'

'Shall we go indoors? Ana will be waiting to serve dinner.'

She needed to freshen up, and use the bathroom. 'Give me ten minutes.'

Elise took time to change into silk trousers and a matching top, then ran a brush through her hair. A quick slash of pink restored colour to her lips.

Her expression was vaguely pensive as she joined Alejandro in the dining-room, and she spooned her soup with little real appetite and merely picked at the tender beef with its accompanying vegetables.

'Not hungry?'

Elise looked at him carefully, examining the strong bone-structure, the assemblage of muscle and skin that moulded his features into compelling attractiveness.

Before the accident she would not have had the least compunction about beginning an argument with him. Not only that, she would have delighted in doing battle, exulting when she succeeded in rousing his temper. It was madness, because she could never win against him.

Now she seemed hell-bent on following a similar path. His brand of caring during their time together at Palm Beach, his tender affection, had wreaked havoc with her emotional heart. Worse, it had destroyed the very core of her resentment.

'No,' she answered at last, pushing her plate to one side.

'Have some fruit.'

Elise looked at the selection Ana had placed in the bowl, then shook her head. She reached for her glass, miscalculated, and water pooled across the table.

'Oh, hell,' she said shakily as she collected a napkin and began mopping up the excess. What was wrong with her, for heaven's sake?

'Leave it.'

She rose to her feet. 'I'll get another napkin.'

'Leave it, Elise,' Alejandro commanded silkily. Stupid tears pricked her eyes, and she blinked furiously in an effort to prevent them from spilling over. Any second now she'd make a fool of herself, and that would never do.

She moved from the table and had taken three steps when a hand closed over her arm.

'Let me go. Please,' she begged in bleak despair, hating the degree of vulnerability evident as he tilted her chin.

'When you tell me what is disturbing you.'

She closed her eyes against the sight of him, then slowly opened them again. 'I didn't deliberately stay in the city in order to cause you concern.'

'I wasn't aware I implied that you had.' He cupped her face between both hands and brushed a thumb-pad across one cheek.

Dear heaven, why did she feel so acutely sensitive where he was concerned? A few days ago she wouldn't have thought it possible that she would find it imperative to offer him any explanation or proffer an apology. Now she was doing both.

However, soul-searching wouldn't achieve anything, for there was no easy resolution.

'Thanks for the car,' she managed unevenly, and glimpsed his faint smile as he watched the fleeting emotions chase across her expressive features.

'What good manners you have, *mi mujer*,' he drawled. 'I shall look forward to a more—passionate shall we say?—expression of your gratitude.'

It took considerable effort to keep the pain from her voice. 'Payment in sexual favours?' she queried, and saw his eyes darken.

'You little fool,' Alejandro responded with deadly softness as his mouth fastened over hers in a kiss that was meant to punish.

A silent cry of impassioned entreaty remained locked in her throat, and it seemed an age before he lifted his head.

His eyes speared hers, and she became trapped beneath the degree of latent sensuality evident, a primeval recognition that had everything to do with the senses.

Her mouth quivered, its soft curves faintly swollen from the ruthless force of his own, and she cried out a single negation as he swept her effortlessly into his arms.

In the bedroom he let her slide down to her feet, and she wanted to vent her rage against his deliberate seduction as he gently cupped her face.

Eyes that were impossibly slumberous held her own captive, and helpless frustration welled up inside her as she became caught up in mesmerised fascination.

Did he know how difficult it was for her to accept the traitorous desire she experienced in his arms? The breath seemed to catch in her throat, and her eyes clung to his, bright with anger, yet intensely vulnerable.

A hand slid beneath her hair, urging her close as his lips trailed across her forehead, then moved slowly down one cheek to settle at the corner of her mouth, teasing, gentle, and incredibly erotic as he conducted a sensual tasting that made her ache for more.

Beneath his sensual mastery a deep flame flared into vibrant life, and she gave herself up totally to the delights of unbridled ardency.

Elise made no protest when he set about freeing her clothes and his own, and her body arched of its own accord as his mouth began a supplicating path over every inch of her body.

She was barely conscious of the tiny sounds emerging from her throat as she began to plead with him, wanting, needing his total possession.

When at last he gave it, she cried out, welcoming his mouth on hers with hungry passion as acute sensation spiralled towards a mutual climax that explored the heights of primitive satiation.

Sexual ecstasy at its zenith, she accepted drowsily a long time later as she drifted towards sleep.

CHAPTER EIGHT

ELISE revelled in her independence, and chose to take the Mercedes out each day.

On one occasion she visited the ward where she had worked at the Royal Children's Hospital, after which she drove by the old brick house she had shared for years with her father.

It looked different, she reflected with a tinge of sadness. The small front garden no longer existed, the curtains had been changed, and the door was now painted a brilliant green.

Was it only nine months since her world had been turned upside-down? In some ways it seemed much longer than that.

It was impossible not to ponder what her future might hold, and that of her unborn child. She wanted... What *did* she want? Alejandro's love? Was it such an impossible dream?

The blast of a car horn interrupted her thoughts, and she set the Mercedes moving away from a street that no longer held a place in her life.

Lunch, she decided, feeling suddenly hungry, after which she would head towards Double Bay to browse among the many boutiques. She might even visit a beauty salon and indulge in a facial. Then she could look for a suitable gown to wear to an important end-of-year function to be held the following evening in an inner-city hotel.

After an extensive search she discovered exactly what she wanted, added matching evening shoes and bag, and tried not to blench as she signed the credit slip.

Alejandro's appreciation of her choice was plainly evident as she bore his appraisal mere minutes before they were due to leave the house the next evening.

'I won't be able to let you out of my sight,' he drawled, and she proffered a teasing smile.

'Likewise.'

'Indeed?'

His eyes held latent passion, and something she dared not define. A tiny flame flared deep within and flowed through her body. 'Shall we leave?'

'So many beautiful women,' Elise murmured as they entered the hotel ballroom some thirty minutes later. 'Wearing a fortune in clothes and jewellery in a personal quest to outshine one another.'

Alejandro cast her an amused glance as one of several hostesses hurried forward to check their tickets and indicate their table position.

'Careful, *querida*,' he drawled. 'Your claws are showing.'

She offered him a winsome smile. 'It's one thing to show them, and quite another to use them.' Unlike Savannah, who didn't hesitate to do both, she added silently as she paused at Alejandro's side while he exchanged pleasantries with an acquaintance.

The ballroom had the capacity to seat eight hundred patrons, with ten guests assigned to each circular table. An impressive annual event, it was a draw for the city's social élite who came primarily to be seen. The promoted charity, the reason for such a gathering, was incidental.

Perhaps that was being a little unkind, Elise decided as she took her seat a short while later. Committee members affiliated to any charity organisation worked tirelessly to put something like this evening's soirée together, and deserved an accolade for their efforts.

Two seats at their table remained empty, and Elise's fingers tightened on the stem of her glass as she overheard who was due to join them.

'Savannah is always late, darling. She likes to make a grand entrance.'

Savannah's presence tonight was a foregone conclusion, but only someone with a twisted sense of humour would have placed the glamorous model at the same table as Alejandro and Elise Santanas. It was too contrived to be coincidental, and Elise could only conclude that Savannah herself had engineered the seating arrangements.

The lights dimmed, a spotlight hit the podium, and the charity's president extolled the amount raised and its purpose. Tonight's guest speaker was a well-known dignitary who would begin his speech at the dinner's conclusion, after which music would be provided for guests to dance.

The spotlight faded, the lights returned, and there was Savannah, looking absolutely stunning in jade silk that clung lovingly to every curve. The man at her side wasn't someone Elise had previously met, and she pinned a smile firmly in place as Savannah performed an introduction.

Was it her imagination that their table was the cynosure of all eyes? Perhaps not, she conceded, although there could be no doubt Savannah's presence would be viewed with interest.

'Elise. How are you? Quite recovered from your accident, I hope?' The slightly bored tone was offset by a seemingly sincere smile which did not reach her eyes as Elise made a polite rejoinder. 'Alejandro missed you dreadfully at last week's dinner.' The smile deepened and became deliberately secretive as she switched attention. 'Didn't you, darling? Quite the devoted husband. If he hadn't been a featured guest speaker, I doubt if he would have come.'

Elise was saved from having to respond by the arrival of a waiter bearing a basket of bread rolls, and when the first course was served she dutifully spooned the delectable potato and leek soup until it was finished.

Faced with a choice of fish or chicken, she opted for the former, and forked each mouthful with studied care. Every so often she paused to sip iced water from her glass, acutely conscious of Savannah's presence directly opposite.

Incredibly beautiful: there was no visible flaw in any one of her perfect features. Nature had bestowed with a bountiful hand, while good fortune had ensured that she'd been born into wealth. A modelling opportunity had landed in her lap at a tender age, and the rest, as they said, was history.

Elise had viewed her with extreme caution the moment they had first met, and nothing had occurred in the interim to change her mind. The model was an ensnarer of men, making it very plain that Alejandro Santanas was her prime target. His marriage was dismissed as of little account, merely a mild irritation soon to be dispensed with.

'Some wine, my dear?'

Elise turned towards the man seated on her left, and shook her head. 'It's kind of you to offer, but no.'

'You're getting by with water, darling?' Savannah queried, effecting a faint *moue*. 'Are you driving?'

Alejandro shifted slightly in his chair and caught hold of Elise's hand, lifting it to his lips. His eyes gleamed with warmth as he gently kissed each fingertip in turn before enfolding her hand in his.

She wanted to wrench her hand free, but even as the thought occurred, his own hand tightened measurably in silent warning, and she had no recourse but to smile. Damn him, he was little more than an elegant savage behind that sophisticated façade. Ruthless, she added, suppressing a slight shiver as she caught sight of Savannah's fixed stare.

'You're not *pregnant*, are you, darling?'

Only Savannah would ask such a question, and Elise held her breath as Alejandro met the model's seemingly innocent gaze.

'Yes, much to my delight.' There was no doubt about the element of steel beneath the silk-smoothness of his voice.

The arrival of dessert was an anticlimax, and Elise picked segments of fruit from their meringue nest, then pushed the plate to one side, choosing tea as the guest speaker took the podium.

Afterwards a DJ provided background music and encouraged guests to step on to the dance-floor. Savannah and her partner were among the first, moving through the steps with effortless ease.

She looked so—sophisticated, and so very sure of herself. Her features were faintly sultry, and Elise had no doubt that the model knew precisely the effect she was having on her partner.

The question was whether it was having the desired effect on Alejandro.

Elise cast him a surreptitious glance, and was disconcerted to meet his hooded gaze. She offered a tentative smile, afraid he might have deduced the pattern of her thoughts, and she blinked as he reached out and threaded his fingers through her own.

'Would you like to dance?'

Part of her wanted to quite desperately, for she badly needed the sanctuary of his embrace. The other part recognised the danger of having her body pressed against the hard powerful impact of his own.

With a word of assent she rose to her feet, moved out on to the floor and into his arms.

The music was slow, and her steps matched his in perfect unison. Magic, she mused. Was it possible for one human being to be addicted to another? Held in thrall as if the essence of him were some powerful narcotic?

He diminished every other man in the room, possessing an inherent ruthlessness, honed by experience and enhanced by the degree of his success.

It held a fascination that men recognised and women viewed with the speculative interest of their sex. To some it was an invisible magnet, activated by the excitement of discovering if the man, freed from corporate restraint, was as skilled at lovemaking as he was at adding millions to his investment portfolio.

An immensely sophisticated man, yet there was the hint of an untamed quality, a primitive savagery held rigidly in control.

A faint shiver feathered down her spine with the knowledge that he would be devastatingly heartless as an enemy.

'Cold?'

His voice was a soft caress against her hair, and she murmured a faint negative.

'Someone just walked over my grave,' she offered, with a droll attempt at humour.

'Savannah?'

She missed a step, and gave an inaudible gasp as he enfolded her close against him. It was a far from conventional hold, and she tilted her head to meet the dark inscrutability apparent in his gaze.

'You're too astute for your own good,' she offered in a strangled voice.

'Is that a disadvantage?'

She chose not to answer, and when the music changed she moved back a pace and suggested they return to their table.

'I need to use the powder-room,' she murmured, aware of the effect of several glasses of water. She caught up her evening bag with the intention of doing a few running repairs to her make-up while there.

'Do you want me to escort you?'

She directed at him a slow smile of amusement. 'I'm not a child, Alejandro. What can happen to me?'

What, indeed? she could only query silently several minutes later, when she emerged from a stall to find Savannah examining her make-up in front of the long mirrored wall.

'Playing to win, darling?' Savannah queried softly.

'Every time, Savannah,' she managed evenly as she took out lipstick and ran colour smoothly over her lips.

'You're very... small,' Savannah opined with a total lack of graciousness. 'A petite size eight?'

There had to be a purpose to this conversation, and determining her dress size was totally irrelevant, Elise reflected as she recapped the lipstick and turned to face her aggressor.

'Alejandro is so...' Savannah trailed off delicately.

'Well-endowed?' Elise suggested, deliberately manufacturing a stunningly amused smile. 'A distinct advantage, wouldn't you agree?'

Dark brown eyes glittered with dangerous venom as the model released a tinkle of soft laughter. 'He's a lusty animal, darling.' Her gaze focused on Elise's trim waist. 'Pregnancy is hardly flattering, especially in the latter stage. I can't imagine he'll practise celibacy, no matter how temporary.'

'And you'll be there for him to turn to?'

'Of course, darling.' She paused, then sharpened the verbal barb for maximum impact. 'As I have been, and always will be.'

Elise felt sickened, and it took considerable effort to summon a light smile. 'I really must go back to the table.' She turned away, only to give an anguished gasp as Savannah caught hold of her injured hand.

'Don't underestimate me.'

'I never have,' Elise assured steadfastly. 'Will you please let go of my hand? It's still quite painful.'

Savannah's grip momentarily tightened, and her eyes gleamed with a malevolence that changed her features into a hard mask.

For a few shocking seconds Elise thought she wouldn't be able to cope with the pain, then Savannah flung her hand aside with a pitiless laugh.

'I'd hate to hurt you unnecessarily.' Collecting her evening bag, she swept out of the powder-room.

For several minutes Elise was locked into immobility as she tried to control her shaken emotions. Her hand throbbed, aching with an intensity that clouded her eyes and took the colour from her face.

'Are you all right?'

The light feminine voice held concern, and Elise dredged up a faint smile.

'You're very pale. Perhaps you should sit down for a few minutes? Shall I fetch your husband?'

'No. No,' she reiterated quickly. 'I'll be all right in a few minutes.'

'My table is next to yours. We'll walk back together, shall we?'

Elise was supremely conscious of Alejandro's intent gaze as she resumed her seat. To her relief there was no sign of Savannah or her partner.

'Would you like more tea?'

She doubted if she would be able to drink it. 'I've had enough, thanks.' In more ways than one, she added silently.

'Do you want to go home?' His voice was quiet, and there was no escaping his penetrating appraisal.

'Not yet,' she managed with commendable calm. To leave now would amount to an admission of defeat, and she was damned if she would give Savannah the satisfaction.

Most of the guests were drifting from one table to another, and Elise gave an inward sigh of relief when another couple joined them. The man, a business associate of Alejandro's, launched into an in-depth discussion with him, while the woman engaged Elise in innocuous conversation.

It was twenty minutes before they left, and Elise cast Alejandro a startled glance as he leaned an arm across the back of her chair.

'It's almost eleven. We've done our duty. Shall we leave?'

'If you want to.'

Without a further word he made their excuses, then began leading the way from the ballroom. Several acquaintances sought his attention and, although he paused momentarily to offer a few words in polite response, he didn't linger.

It was a relief to reach the car, and once inside Elise simply leaned back against the leather-cushioned seat as Alejandro eased the Bentley up to street level and into the steady stream of traffic vacating the city.

Her hand still throbbed, although with less intensity, and the pain had subsided to a deep nagging ache. Bearable, she conceded, but only just.

Music emitted from the stereo speakers, and she closed her eyes as the car sped smoothly towards Point Piper.

Once indoors she made straight for the stairs, discarding her clothes as she entered the bedroom. When Alejandro appeared, only a bra and briefs shielded her from total nudity.

'Want to tell me what upset you?'

Her eyes held a hint of defiance. 'Not really.'

'Savannah followed you into the powder-room, and emerged minutes ahead of you.'

'How observant of you to notice.'

He crossed to stand within touching distance. 'I notice everything about you,' he drawled, sliding a hand beneath her hair to cup her nape. 'The way you respond when we make love. What makes you smile. How your eyes cloud with pain,' he said quietly.

'Savannah and I exchanged a few words.' She attempted a shrug, and met his gaze unflinchingly. 'Is there any reason why we shouldn't?'

His eyes darkened fractionally. 'None at all.' His hand slid forward, and his thumb caressed the soft outline of her mouth.

His touch was an erotic force, and she fought an inner battle not to succumb to his subtle brand of foreplay as he reached to unclasp her bra, freeing her breasts from the scrap of silk and lace.

The burgeoning peaks ached for his touch, and a faint moan escaped her throat as he stroked the creamy fullness before paying attention to each dusky peak.

His hands slid down her ribcage, over her waist to slip beneath her briefs, carrying them down over her hips with effortless ease before transferring his attention as he removed his own clothes.

Then he reached for her, both hands framing her face as he lowered his head.

His mouth was an erotic instrument, and she welcomed his kiss without reserve, exulting in the liquid warmth coursing through her veins. Her whole body seemed alive with acute sensation, and she moved close against him, needing the physical contact. Most of all she wanted to be swept away by primitive desire, to become so lost in the rapture of his lovemaking that Savannah and her hateful words would be pushed beyond the periphery of rational thought.

It was almost as if he knew, and a low groan of delighted anticipation emerged from her throat as he drew her down on to the bed and began conducting a leisurely tasting of every sensual pleasure-spot.

She exulted in the degree of eroticism he skilfully bestowed, the depth of emotion she experienced beneath his touch, so that when he finally took her it was all she could do not to cry out with joy.

Afterwards she lay curled into the curve of his body, delightfully sated and on the verge of sleep.

Elise woke later to find that Alejandro had already left for the city, and she indulged in a leisurely stretch before sliding from the bed. So far she had been very fortunate, for, although she occasionally experienced a slight queasiness on waking, it had not developed into morning sickness.

After a refreshing shower she dressed in shorts and a top, then ran lightly downstairs to the kitchen.

'Morning, Ana. Isn't it a beautiful day?'

'*Sí*,' the older woman answered with a warm smile. 'I will get your breakfast.'

'I'll do it.' Cereal, fruit and toast, with orange juice and tea, were simple enough to assemble. Besides, she'd looked after herself for years, and valued a degree of independence.

Elise enjoyed a leisurely breakfast, browsing through the morning papers, then when she had finished she moved outside for a walk round the gardens.

The flowers were beautiful, grown in colour coordinated borders that were a visual delight: delicate pinks and whites, brilliant reds and yellows, then carefully clipped shrubs. There were a number of urns gracing the steps leading down from the terrace, and a splendid concrete tiered bird-bath was the central feature of a square expanse of manicured lawn.

Beyond that lay the swimming-pool with an adjacent cabana which housed a bar and changing-rooms.

It was a magnificent property, the architecture and landscaping in perfect harmony. Its location and beautiful views out over the harbour indicated a value she was hesitant to calculate.

Was it any wonder that Savannah coveted the man who owned it? His position in the city's social scene was unquestionable, and there were few women who were not fascinated by rich and powerful men. Some even sold themselves in a quest for fame and fortune.

As she had. Although not for fame or fortune. Her father... Dammit, such introspection was dangerous. It led nowhere, and achieved nothing except to highlight her own insecurities.

Love was a mixture of heaven and hell. Especially when you were not loved in return. The physicalities of lovemaking were there, but not the emotional commitment.

Would it ever be any different? *Could* it be? Sadly, she didn't think so.

Elise wandered down to the swimming-pool and sat in one of the chairs positioned beneath a wide sun-umbrella. The sun felt warm against her bare skin, and she leaned her head back and closed her eyes.

'Elise? It is ten-fifteen.'

She came sharply awake at the sound of Ana's voice, amazed that she could have lapsed into a light doze.

Her hand had swollen slightly and was beginning to show signs of bruising. There was also a degree of pain when the physiotherapist supervised her exercises, a fact which he noted, adding an admonition to be more careful. There didn't seem much point in assuring him that it was not self-inflicted.

At home she ate the chicken salad Ana had prepared for lunch, then she changed into a bikini, selected a book, and wandered out to sit beneath a shade-umbrella by the pool.

It was almost six when Alejandro arrived home, and Elise cast him a warm smile as he entered the lounge.

'How was your day?' she asked lightly, and was unprepared for his brief hard kiss.

'A series of meetings, appointments.' His tone was dry, his eyes dark and inscrutable. 'I'll change. Then we'll have a drink before dinner.'

'I'll go and check with Ana.'

The table was already set, and there was a delicious aroma emanating from the kitchen.

'Vegetable soup,' Ana informed her as she stirred the contents of a saucepan. 'Paella, with fresh fruit to finish.'

'Sounds wonderful. Can I help with anything?'

'It is all under control,' the older woman beamed companionably. 'I will serve in fifteen minutes.'

Elise wandered towards the lounge, and was busy watching the televised news when Alejandro entered the room.

He looked vaguely satanic in casual dark trousers and a polo shirt which highlighted the olive tint of his skin and emphasised his length and breadth. 'A cool drink?'

She glanced towards him and her breath caught in her throat as she glimpsed the hard demeanour just beneath the surface of his control. 'Please,' she managed evenly, returning her attention to the television.

She turned as he reached her side, and instead of handing her a glass he placed both down on a nearby pedestal.

'Let me see your hand.'

He knew. *How*? The physiotherapist? There was no one else who could have told him, she reasoned silently.

'It's a bit stiff,' she admitted with a helpless shrug, unwilling to extend it for his inspection.

'Some bruising, pain and reduced mobility,' Alejandro stated with dangerous softness, 'consistent with the hand being compressed.' He reached forward and carefully caught hold of her arm. His intent examination filled her with a peculiar sense of dread, and she almost died at the savagery apparent as he seared her features. 'Savannah?'

She swallowed nervously. 'What if I accidentally knocked my hand?'

His expression became inscrutable, and his voice contained dangerous indolence. 'Did you?'

Evasion of the truth was hardly wise, for there was already visible evidence of bruising. 'No.'

He said something vicious beneath his breath in Spanish, then lifted a hand to cup her jaw. His finger traced a gentle pattern over her lower lip, probing slightly before moving to caress her cheek. His eyes became dark, their depths unfathomable as he searched her features.

'My relationship with Savannah was...' He paused fractionally, then said deliberately, 'Mutually convenient.'

Mutual need, Elise qualified, sickened at the picture that conjured up.

'Marriage was not something I had considered until you stormed into my office in a state of fury and began hurling accusations and making allegations.' His smile held wry cynicism. 'Over dinner that same evening I decided I wanted your loyalty, your fierce pride, your honesty.'

He had deliberately tested her, and it rankled unbearably.

He brushed her mouth lightly with his own. 'Eventually—your love,' he added quietly.

He had placed the chess-pieces on a board, and played the game with infinite patience and skill. She hurt too much to let him know that he had won.

'Along with good health, love is something that money can't buy,' Elise declared carefully, and glimpsed a flicker of pain in the depths of his eyes, so fleeting that she wondered if she had imagined it.

'The time between being informed of your accident and discovering the extent of your injuries were the worst minutes I have ever spent,' he assured her ruminatively as he took possession of her mouth in a kiss so incredibly gentle that she simply closed her eyes and gave herself up to the sensual eroticism of his touch.

It seemed an age before he broke contact and slowly lifted his head.

It took enormous will-power to step away from him, and her voice was not quite steady as she offered, 'Ana will be ready to serve dinner.'

'Then let us go in and cat.'

CHAPTER NINE

IT WAS a week later that Elise entered the elegant Double Bay salon and checked with Reception.

'Raphael will be five minutes, Elise,' the stunning blonde told her with a bright smile. 'He's running a little late. Perhaps you'd care to take a seat? Would you like some tea or coffee? Orange juice, mineral water?'

Elise shook her head in silent negation, adding a polite, 'Thanks,' before selecting a chair.

A year ago—make that nine months ago, she corrected mentally—she wouldn't have been able to afford to walk into this exclusive hairdressing salon. To have had Raphael himself apply his artistic cutting expertise to her hair would have been unthinkable.

The name Santanas opened doors, commanded respect, and produced a desire to pander to any whim with such obsequious effusiveness that it was almost obscene.

Elise reached for one of several thick glossy magazines and began flipping through the pages, noting the elegant models, the beautiful clothes, designer make-up, articles written in stylish prose, a feature profile on one of Australia's social doyennes, another profile on a top designer, and the usual society pages with a run-down on recent events with accompanying photographs.

She skimmed over them without interest, only to be riveted by a frame depicting Alejandro with Savannah at his side.

Her stomach gave a painful lurch, and she took a deep breath as she willed herself to check the magazine's date of issue. The event highlighted was a dinner organised specifically to raise money for a well-known charity.

Oh, hell. Why did she have to pick *that* particular magazine? She could have remained in ignorance. Besides, she silently attempted to reassure herself, the photograph was probably the result of coincidence, taken when Savannah just happened to be standing at his side.

And pigs might fly, she added mentally. There was nothing innocent in any one of Savannah's actions. The way Savannah was gazing at him in open adoration was positively sickening.

'Elise. How are you, darling? Sorry to keep you waiting.'

She closed the magazine and rose to her feet with a ready smile. 'Raphael.'

An extrovert, he delighted in the portrayal of exaggerated mannerisms, creating an erroneous image that was in direct contrast to his true personality. White harem-style trousers and a fine white muslin artist's shirt with numerous tiny pleats fanning out from a deep yoke gave the illusion of adding to his lean frame. A diamond stud adorned one ear, he wore a diamond signet ring on his left hand, and a religious medallion suspended from a thick chain hung low against his chest. Long black hair was sleekly plastered against his scalp and caught together at his nape to form a ponytail.

'Your hand? It is still giving you pain?' He drew her towards the far end of the salon and seated her at a basin.

'It aches a little.'

Raphael's personal attention was rare, and Elise, by virtue of being Alejandro's wife, appeared to be one of the favoured few.

She wrinkled her nose as he sluiced water over her hair and applied shampoo, rinsed and repeated the process with conditioner, then towelled it dry before leading her to a mirrored cubicle.

'You are able to drive again?'

'The specialist says I can. Alejandro would prefer José to continue in the role of chauffeur. Although he has compromised and bought me another car.'

'He is being protective, hmm?'

'You could say that,' she agreed with suitable dryness.

Raphael picked up his scissors and comb, and went to work. 'Don't knock it, darling,' he cautioned wryly. 'Men are not usually protective unless they care.'

Alejandro's brand of caring was linked to their unborn child. *She* was merely a secondary consideration.

Or was she? From the beginning his lovemaking had generated a desire for her pleasure as much as his own, and there had never been an occasion when she had felt—*used*.

When had she fallen in love with him? Sadly, Elise couldn't pinpoint a single moment when the revelation had hit. She was aware only of its stealthy possession, and the agonising knowledge that her life would never be the same without him.

'Tonight is the exhibition of fine art held in one of the Woollahra Galleries,' Raphael informed her. 'You are attending, of course.'

Alejandro was a known patron of the arts, and he had a reputation for adding one or two paintings each year to his collection of works by Australian artists.

The evening's event included cocktails and hors-d'oeuvres, and attendance was strictly by invitation.

'Yes.'

'A notable occasion,' Raphael proffered as his scissors moved with crafted expertise.

Without doubt, she agreed mentally. The social glitterati would be present, together with members of the Press, and several photographers, each attempting to outdo the other.

She had even bought a new black gown. Sleeveless, its simple slim-fitting style was enhanced with intricate silver embroidery on the bodice. A high scooped neckline precluded jewellery, and there were matching shoes and evening bag.

Raphael reached for several fat rollers and positioned them in place, collected a magazine for her to read, then moved towards Reception to greet the next client.

It was almost four when Elise emerged, another half-hour before she brought the Mercedes to a halt beside the main entrance of Alejandro's Point Piper home.

She could hear the shower running as she entered their suite, and she stripped down to briefs and bra, collected a silk robe and slipped it on, then she crossed to the dressing-table to attend to her make-up.

Alejandro entered the bedroom, with a towel hitched low on his hips, as she applied the finishing touches, and she watched in mesmerised fascination as he moved to her side and bestowed a lingering kiss on the soft curve of her neck.

His touch sent warmth tingling through her veins, and her expression held a faint wistfulness as he stood behind her and viewed their mirrored reflections.

'What time do you want to leave?' she queried, unable to tear her gaze away.

'Fifteen minutes. The traffic will be heavy.' His hands rested on her shoulders, then slowly slid down the front edges of her robe to slip beneath the silk and gently tease the softness of her breasts. With tantalising care he began to brush the pad of his thumb over each sensitive peak.

Elise felt them swell and harden, and she gave a soundless gasp as his fingers slid to unfasten her bra.

'Alejandro——'

'Humour me,' he said huskily. His eyes held hers captive, their depths alive with leashed passion. 'I have thought of little else all day. The intoxicating texture of your skin, its delicate perfume, the way your beautiful eyes soften when I touch you.'

Sensation spiralled from her feminine core as intense sexual awareness swept through her body. All he had to do was pull her into his arms and she would be lost.

'Shouldn't we get ready?' she asked in a strangled voice, and glimpsed the edge of his mouth twist in a gesture of wry self-mockery.

'Indeed.' His hands lingered, then slowly withdrew to settle briefly on her shoulders. 'If I kiss you, we'll never leave this room.'

'In that case, perhaps you'd better get changed and let me finish my make-up,' she suggested shakily, and he laughed, a deep, soft, husky sound that sent goose-bumps over the surface of her skin.

'Eventually we will return home, *mi mujer*, and then we shall resume where we have left off.'

'If I'm not too tired.' It was a tame attempt at denial, and didn't fool him in the least.

'I promise to do all the work, *querida*.' His lips brushed her temple, then slid down to nibble an earlobe.

Not all, she promised silently as he moved away and selected underwear, a dress-shirt and black trousers that formed parts of a sophisticated shield for the primitive strength of his body. Socks, shoes came next, and when he reached for the immaculate bow tie she hurriedly transferred her attention and picked up a shiny gold tube with which to stroke pastel colour on to her lips.

Her choice of perfume was her favourite, Evelyn, a subtle rose fragrance that imbued the skin with immense delicacy.

Five minutes later she slipped into the gown, and she stood perfectly still as Alejandro slid the zip-fastener into place.

'You look beautiful,' he complimented as she stepped into the elegant evening shoes.

Collecting her evening bag, she turned towards him and proffered a faint smile. 'The women will vie with each other for your attention,' she anticipated lightly.

'I have no control over inherited genes,' he responded in an amused drawl. 'And the only woman I am interested in is you.'

For now, Elise added silently, wishing she could believe him. It would be incredible to feel truly secure in a man's love, to know without any element of doubt that you were adored, and that even if he displayed visual appreciation for another no other woman had a chance of capturing his heart.

Such a hope belonged in the realms of fantasy, she decided ruefully, as the Bentley became part of the flow of traffic entering the inner-city perimeter.

Reality was a combination of harsh facts and formidable statistics which existed as irrefutable proof that love did not always last forever. The first heady bloom often flared brilliantly, only to diminish all too frequently to a state of prosaic affection.

The car slid to a halt, and Elise's eyes widened with the realisation that they were stationary. The car park was brightly lit, and there were sounds and movement as guests vacated their cars.

Alejandro caught her elbow in a light clasp and led her towards the main entrance. Inside, several guests mingled in small groups, and there were several smartly uniformed waiters and waitresses proffering drinks and bite-sized food.

Almost at once Alejandro was greeted by the gallery owner and engaged in conversation, and Elise found herself drawn into a civilised debate on the advantages of free artistic expression over the confines of conformity.

'Do you enjoy Alejandro's artistic taste?'

Oh, hell, she wasn't even sure which artists he favoured. The paintings hanging on the walls at Point Piper and Palm Beach were visually pleasing, although a few were a little too modern for her own enjoyment.

'Mostly,' she agreed. 'Although he has a Pro Hart of which I'm not particularly fond.'

'My wife is a traditionalist,' Alejandro relayed smoothly. 'Her taste runs to Max Boyd.'

'Oh, my dear. Hart is quite brilliant.'

'So are a number of other noted Australian artists,' she offered firmly. 'It's very much a personal choice, don't you think?'

'There's an excellent piece you really must see. Expensive, but worthy of investment.' He riffled through the catalogue pages and brought the item to Alejandro's notice, then made his excuses as someone else demanded his attention.

'I happen to like Max Boyd,' Elise protested as Alejandro's amused gaze rested on her expressive features.

'So do I,' he assured her, and, placing an arm round her waist, he directed her towards a display. 'Shall we begin viewing?'

Some paintings verged on the bizarre, others resembled caricatures of design over brilliant slashes of colour. One in particular looked as if a child at kindergarten level had indulged in a totally wild battle with numerous pots of multi-coloured paint.

'What do you think?'

Elise turned towards Alejandro and endeavoured to present a considered viewpoint. After several seconds she voiced with restraint, 'I'd prefer not to answer on the grounds that anything I say could be overheard, taken into account, and held against me.'

'A remarkable nonconformist piece,' Alejandro drawled knowledgeably, and her eyes danced as she nodded in silent agreement. 'Shall we move on?'

'Please.'

There were a number of guests present whom she had met before, and for the next hour she exchanged pleasantries, accepted an invitation for an upcoming fashion parade, deferred to Alejandro on no less than three dinner invitations, and she was just beginning to find the evening a relaxing venture when she glimpsed a familiar head several feet distant.

Savannah. As if by design the guests shifted position so that the model's body profile was in clear view: a stunning figure, attired in a flamboyant gown that on anyone one else would have looked totally outrageous.

Elise forced herself to meet Savannah's intent gaze, and for one brief second she witnessed unadulterated venom before it was masked. A slight smile appeared in acknowledgement before Savannah turned towards her partner, and Elise was unable to prevent a slight shiver.

Did Alejandro know Savannah was here? It was a distinct probability.

'More mineral water?'

'Thank you.'

'We should be able to get away in less than an hour. We'll go on to dinner afterwards,' Alejandro said quietly.

'Have you already booked?'

He named a well-known restaurant famed for its fine cuisine. 'You would prefer somewhere else?'

'Quiet, out of the way, with little chance of meeting anyone we know?' she suggested hopefully.

'I can recollect a few.'

Suitable for clandestine meetings? Damn, she had to stop resorting to destructive introspection! 'Of course, we could buy a take-away meal on the way home.'

'Anything in particular?'

'Chinese?'

His eyes gleamed with humour. 'I'll cancel the restaurant from the car.'

'Thank you.'

He lifted a hand and brushed his fingers lightly across her cheek. 'Just where precisely do you intend we eat?'

She looked at him with undue solemnity. 'Dressed like this?' she enquired innocently. 'At the dining-room table. Where else?'

'We could always change first.'

'And eat out on the terrace?' She offered a singularly sweet smile. 'What a wonderful idea.'

The depths of his eyes took on a dark brilliance. 'Minx. Remind me to extract due penance.'

'You wouldn't dare.'

A slow, wicked smile tugged the edges of his mouth, and his voice held infinite indolence. 'Just watch me.'

Every bone in her body began to feel liquefied at the thought of precisely how he would exact atonement. 'I think,' she said unsteadily, 'we should attempt to continue our viewing, don't you?'

'An excellent suggestion.'

It was after eight when they left, and almost nine before Alejandro garaged the car. The plastic carrier bag with its various containers emitted a mouth-watering aroma, and Elise slid off her shoes the moment they entered the house.

'You intend to change before we eat?'

She cast him a studied glance. 'This gown cost a small fortune.'

'So did my suit,' drawled Alejandro.

'Perhaps you should exchange it for something less formal.'

'And save on the dry-cleaning bill?'

'Naturally.'

'I gather eating in bed would be considered the height of decadence?'

She failed miserably in suppressing an impish smile. 'It would be such a shame to waste the food.'

'The terrace?'

Her eyes twinkled with devilish humour. 'Think of the moonlight.'

He shrugged out of his jacket and placed it over a nearby chair. 'Plates, cutlery, glasses?'

She pretended due consideration. 'I guess we could opt for informality,' she decided as she picked up her shoes and made for the staircase. 'Two forks, two glasses.' She began mounting the stairs, then paused to look down at him. 'Do you think you can manage that?'

He removed the bow tie and loosened the top buttons on his shirt. 'Don't be too long, *querida*,' he warned gently, and her mouth curved into a guileless smile.

'Patience, Alejandro.' She turned and slowly traversed the remaining stairs. In the bedroom she slipped out of the gown, then dressed in silk culottes and a loose top.

Minutes later she walked out on to the terrace to find Alejandro seated at one of the outdoor tables, a portable lamp providing essential light, the food displayed in its various containers, and a slim flute of wine within easy reach. His shirt was undone almost to the waist, the cuffs rolled halfway up his forearms.

Elise sank into a chair opposite, dipped a fork into chop suey, and savoured a mouthful with suitable enthusiasm, then repeated the process. 'Isn't this better than eating in a restaurant?'

He forked a prawn into his mouth, then shot her a musing look. 'This is quite good.'

'Don't sound so surprised.' She met his gaze and wrinkled her nose at him in admonition. 'The trouble is you've been thoroughly spoilt, with a personal cook and professional chefs to pander to your gourmand taste.'

'Planning to re-educate me, Elise?'

'In some areas it mightn't be a bad idea.'

'And what areas are those, my darling wife?' He sounded distinctly amused, and dangerously indolent.

'You could do with a lesson in humility,' she said with mock severity.

'Where you are concerned, I am remarkably humble,' Alejandro claimed solemnly. His eyes held hers, and she couldn't look away as he lifted his glass in a silent salute before placing the rim to his mouth.

He sounded sincere. Almost as if he cared very much. The breath caught in her throat, and she found it difficult to swallow.

Her fork was suspended in mid-air, and she slowly replaced it on the table, her appetite gone.

He leaned back in the chair, his large frame displaying an indolent grace that was deceptive, for there was a watchfulness apparent, a leashed air she found infinitely disturbing. 'Lost for words, Elise?'

She looked at him for what seemed an age, wanting more than anything to move into his arms, to lift her mouth for his kiss. But she seemed locked into immobility, and there was a strange ache in the region of her heart.

There was so much she wanted to say, yet she felt hesitant, afraid that if she revealed too much it would render her vulnerable.

'Shall I make coffee?' Even her voice sounded breathy and uncertain, and she cursed her own insecurity.

'No coffee,' Alejandro said gently. 'I'll dispose of these containers, then we'll go to bed.'

Bed. That was her downfall. It was where she sold her soul and lost control.

'I'm not tired,' she offered quietly, and glimpsed his faint smile.

'Neither am I. Sleeping wasn't exactly what I had in mind.'

She rose to her feet and gathered up the cutlery and glasses, then carried them through to the kitchen.

Alejandro followed, and she heard him locking the outer doors and setting the security alarm.

It was a simple task to load the dishwasher, and she had just finished when he entered the room.

He looked vaguely piratical: dark trousers, deep olive skin, dark hair, in stark contrast to the white shirt. And tall. He almost seemed overpowering, and, while she craved his touch, there was a part of her that cried out against any sexual subjugation.

She watched as he despatched food down the waste-disposal unit, then dropped empty containers into the pedal-bin before washing and drying his hands.

In silence he turned and caught hold of her hand, leading her through to the lounge, where he selected a compact disc and slid it into the disc player.

Soft music emanated from the speakers and Elise looked at him speechlessly as he drew her into his arms.

Crazy, she thought, as he pulled her close against him and began to drift slowly round the room. She felt his lips brush her hair, followed by the warmth of his breath against her temple. His heartbeat was strong beneath her cheek, and her hands crept to link together at the back of his waist.

The music was so slow and dreamy that after several minutes they hardly bothered to move at all, and simply stood still in the dim light reflected from the foyer.

His kiss was so incredibly gentle that it almost made her cry, and she offered him her mouth, exulting in an erotic tasting that excited without demand.

When the music finished he raised his head and subjected her to a long, searching gaze, then he placed an arm beneath her knees and carried her up the stairs.

Elise wanted to cry, and when he lowered her to her feet in the bedroom, tears shimmered like crystal droplets in each corner of her eyes.

Without a word he led her to the bed and sat down on its edge, then he drew her to stand between his thighs.

Her mouth began to tremble, and there was nothing she could do to prevent the slow downward path of a single tear as it overflowed.

Alejandro lifted a hand and halted its passage with the pad of his thumb before moving to trace the outline of her mouth.

'I was almost hesitant to question the cause,' he drawled gently. 'Do you want to blame it on ambivalent emotions?'

'I guess that's as good a reason as any,' she owned shakily, and almost died at the wealth of passion evident in those dark eyes so close to her own.

'I need you,' he said gently. 'Every day in my life. All night long in my bed.'

Need. Need had to be better than *want*, didn't it? And 'every day in my life' sounded permanent. As in forever?

She wanted to say, '*I love you.*' But the words wouldn't emerge.

He pulled her on to his lap and kissed her, then carefully eased her on to the bed.

Her arms lifted to curve round his neck as she gave herself up to the magic only he was able to create. Soon she was filled with an agonising sweetness as her body began to respond to the exquisite *tendresse* of his touch, and she throbbed with intense awareness when he entered her, glorying in the mutual joy of complete possession as they journeyed towards a mutual fulfilment of the senses.

It was a wild sweet pleasure tempered by raw desire. Erotic, primitive, yet so incredibly sensual she was held captive in its thrall . . . *his* without any equivocation.

On the edge of sleep she was conscious of his arms enfolding her close, and she gave a tiny sigh of contentment before drifting in a dreamless state that lasted until morning.

CHAPTER TEN

'ELISE. There is a telephone call for you.'

Very few calls for her came through the house phone. Alejandro rang direct on the mobile net, likewise the few of her friends to whom she had given the number. Perhaps it was the obstetrician's receptionist rescheduling her appointment.

'Who is it, Ana?'

'Siobhan Barry.'

If Siobhan was calling at this time, it meant she had the day off. Perhaps they could meet for lunch, Elise mused as she crossed to the nearest handset.

'Siobhan. How are you?'

There was a brief silence. '*Savannah*, darling. Did Ana get it wrong?'

A chill feeling settled in the pit of her stomach. Even allowing for misunderstanding, Savannah's surname was vastly dissimilar to that of Siobhan. Which meant Savannah had deliberately set out to deceive. There could be little doubt as to why.

'Is it essential we have this conversation?' Elise managed steadily, and heard a faint intake of breath down the line.

'I suppose you think you're clever,' Savannah opined viciously.

It was a game that had to be played out to its conclusion, Elise decided, saddened that it should have even begun. 'Perhaps you'd care to elaborate.'

'You poisonous little bitch. You had to tell him, didn't you?'

Elise closed her eyes, then slowly opened them again. 'If you're referring to my hand . . . blame the physiotherapist,' she managed carefully, 'and Alejandro, for insisting on a first-hand report every time I visit any member of the medical profession.'

There was a long pause. 'Watch your back, darling.'

'I always do.' Without hesitation she replaced the receiver, only to lift it again and dial a memorised number.

A sleepy voice repeated the digits, and Elise felt a surge of relief. 'Siobhan? How about lunch?'

'I didn't get to bed until three, you impossible person. Must it be today?'

'We could make it a late lunch,' Elise persisted, and heard Siobhan's laughing approval.

'Name the time and place, and I'll meet you there.'

'One-thirty. Doyle's at Watson's Bay,' she returned without hesitation.

They met within minutes of the appointed time, and managed by good fortune to be shown to a table overlooking the beach. After the serious business of ordering was completed, they settled down to exchanging news, something which lasted through the starter, and well into the main course.

'You're positively blooming,' Siobhan complimented quietly. 'Your hair, your skin. Everything
about you. I couldn't be more pleased everything
is working out.'

Elise managed a bright smile that didn't fool her
friend in the slightest.

'Not quite, huh? What's the problem?'

'I didn't ask you to meet me to discuss any
problems.'

'Hell, no. You love my wit, my charm.' She
leaned forward, her expression pensive. 'I refuse to
believe it has anything to do with Alejandro.
Savannah?' she hazarded.

'Why not Alejandro?'

Siobhan shot her an old-fashioned look. 'My
God, you really can't see it, can you?' she queried,
shaking her head in silent disbelief. 'Did you never
wonder why I didn't visit you in hospital?' Her expression sobered. 'Alejandro requested—*requested*,' she insisted, 'I stay away until you
regained your memory.' Her eyes took on an earnest
fervour. 'He rang me every day to let me know how
you were.'

Elise could only look at her in shocked silence.
Why would he do something like that if he didn't
want to make the most of an opportunity to repair
her perception of him? It was crazy. Yet only last
night...

'Go figure, Elise,' Siobhan advised gently. 'And,
if you're still in any doubt, ask yourself why he
insisted on marriage, when it would have been infinitely more simple to install you as his mistress.'

It was almost four when they left the restaurant, and a short while later Elise garaged the car, then moved lightly indoors.

Ana was busy peeling vegetables as she entered the kitchen, and she uttered an appreciative sound as the delicious aroma of roast chicken assailed her nostrils.

'Anything I can do to help?'

Ana's smile, like the woman herself, was warm and friendly. 'Alejandro rang. He will be home early. If you must do something, you could set the table.'

Afterwards she took a long, leisurely shower, then dressed in a white silk blouse and tailored straight skirt. She was putting the finishing touches to her make-up when Alejandro entered the bedroom.

Elise offered him a tentative smile, then concentrated on colouring the lower curve of her mouth. Her eyes widened as she saw his reflected image in the mirror, and she stood perfectly still as he turned her round to face him.

'I had a call from the physiotherapist. It appears you forgot your appointment this afternoon.'

Surprise flitted across her features. Damn, it had completely slipped her mind. 'I'll ring tomorrow and offer my apologies. I met Siobhan for lunch.'

His eyes pierced hers. 'Ana said Siobhan phoned. Strange,' he continued thoughtfully, 'when the only number she has is linked to your personal mobile.'

Elise lifted her hands, then let them fall to her sides in a helpless gesture. 'Savannah rang, and tricked Ana that she was Siobhan, then attempted to have me believe Ana had made a mistake over the name.'

'Do you want to tell me about it?'

'Not particularly.'

'Elise——'

'Don't, Alejandro. Please.' She felt so incredibly vulnerable that if he touched her she would shatter and fall in an ignominious heap at his feet.

Even now, the pain was still there, yet she managed to hold his gaze with dignity. Dared she risk all and reveal how she felt? Expunge the anguish, and pray that Siobhan was right?

Drawing a deep breath, she took courage in both hands and began.

'I need to tell you that I viewed my father's death as a ticket to escape a marriage I considered to have been arranged in hell. The night he lay so ill in hospital, I forgot to take the Pill. Ironic, wouldn't you say, that he should die within hours of my discovering I might be pregnant?' She bit the edge of her lip to prevent it from trembling, and the breath caught in her throat as he lifted both hands to frame her face.

'So you ran.' His thumb traced the edge of her lower lip. She swallowed involuntarily, and his eyes narrowed faintly as he witnessed her nervous reaction.

'I considered I had no choice.'

'*Gracias*, Elise.' There was a bitterness apparent that tore her apart.

There was no doubt he desired her, but desire alone had little to do with need, *love*. 'After the accident,' she began shakily, 'you were always there, the image of a devoted husband.' Her eyes searched his, seeing the darkness apparent, the faint tenseness as he waited for her to continue. 'When my memory returned, I felt betrayed. I had trusted you,' she cried in an anguished whisper.

He was quiet for a long time. 'There was no reason for you to distrust me.'

'You perceived it as a game,' Elise went on with incredible sadness. 'With me as the pawn.'

'From the beginning,' he corrected quietly, 'you were the prize.'

'Prey,' she countered. 'Ruthlessly hunted, and relentlessly lured into a trap.'

His gaze was unwavering, intense, and impossible to read.

'You acted a part,' she accused, and saw his eyes darken.

'Never,' he assured her after a long silence, and her features paled.

'I don't believe you.'

'No? You perceived our lovemaking as a calculated coupling without any depth of emotional involvement?'

It had never been that, not even in the beginning. '*Love* isn't a prerequisite for satisfactory sex.' She felt as if she were breaking up inside, her body slowly shattering with each successive word he uttered.

He was silent for what seemed an age, and his voice when he spoke sounded like silk being sliced by the finest tempered steel. 'You can describe what we share as merely clinical satisfaction?'

She looked at him carefully, seeing the strength apparent, the hint of passion in the depths of those dark eyes. 'No,' she owned at last.

His thumb trailed to her cheekbone, explored the faint hollow beneath, then slid to rest at the corner of her mouth. *'Por Dios,'* he declared huskily. 'An admission.'

Time stood still, and she was willing to swear that her heart stopped beating for several seconds before kicking in at a quickened pace as the pad of his thumb slid halfway along her lower lip to rest there momentarily before gently compressing its fullness.

'And *this,'* he drawled with emphasis, as his hand shaped one sensitised breast, deliberately tracing a provocative pattern back and forth across its aching peak, 'is your body's reaction to the caress of any man?'

Dear God, no. *You,* she vowed silently. Only you.

His eyes were dark, almost black, gleaming like polished onyx as he reached into her mind and so easily read what was there.

'Impossible, of course, for you to comprehend you are the love of my life?'

The silence was so total that she forgot to breathe, then her chest lurched as she drew in the first of several deep ragged gasps of air.

'They're only words, Alejandro,' she managed shakily, wanting desperately to believe them.

'They are all I have left.' His eyes were dark, unguarded, and filled with a depth of passion that made her senses reel.

'Your amnesia provided me with a heaven-sent opportunity to begin afresh. Without the barrier of your animosity, it became possible for you to believe you were the very much loved wife of a man who clearly adored you.' He paused, and his touch was so gentle that it made her want to cry. 'I prayed your memory loss would last long enough for those weeks we had together to make a difference.'

'The baby——'

His finger pressed closed her lips, and his eyes were incredibly dark. 'Make no mistake, *querida*. The child you carry is a wonderful bonus. But it is you I care for. *You.*'

She shivered at the soft invasive pull on her emotions as his fingers slid to her nape and angled her head towards his.

'Please—*don't*,' she whispered in anguish.

His head lowered to hers, and his breath was warm against her lips. 'Why not, *querida*?'

Her stomach lurched, then curled into a painful knot as his mouth brushed hers. She couldn't have moved, even if her limbs had been willing. 'Because I can't think when you do that.'

She sensed rather than glimpsed his smile. 'Is it so important that you *think*?'

The tip of his tongue touched the corner of her mouth, savoured the indentation, then lightly traced the full curve to the centre. Liquid fire coursed through her veins, igniting each separate nerve-end until her body seemed one vibrant entity.

'If I don't,' she managed in strangled tones, 'you'll simply sweep me into oblivion.'

She sensed his smile, and heard the faint husky growl emerge from his throat. 'Would that be so bad?'

His mouth was creating the sweetest magic with her own, a slow, tantalising prelude to what must surely follow, and her body began to heat, every nerve-end flaring into vibrant life as her soul reached out to his.

'Alejandro...' His name escaped her lips in a shaken gasp as he drew her close in against the swollen evidence of his desire.

It was almost as if he needed to absorb her—flesh, bones, the very essence that made her unique—and she could feel herself slowly melting, slipping inevitably down into a glorious pool of swirling warmth where there was only an acute perception of the senses, the sweet promise of two souls perfectly in accord merging and becoming one.

With a sense of desperation she dragged her mouth away from his, aware in a moment of complete lucidity that it was because he allowed it.

Her lips felt soft and swollen, tender, and they trembled slightly beneath the moistness of her tongue as she unconsciously ran its tip along the lower edge.

His eyes flared, watching the movement with mesmerised fascination.

Almost as if he could not restrain himself, he leaned forward and brushed his lips against her temple, then pressed each eyelid closed before trailing down to the edge of her lips. His touch was as light as a butterfly's wing, caressing, loving, and she wanted to cry out against his flagrant seduction.

'I expressed my adoration with the touch of my hands, my mouth...my body,' Alejandro declared. He lapsed into Spanish, then repeated the words softly in a language she understood. Erotic, explicit, undeniably earthy. Yet heartfelt, and without any pretence.

Soft colour flooded her cheeks, and her lips trembled as a low husky chuckle emerged from his throat.

'Have I shocked you?' he mocked gently.

A wicked smile curved her generous mouth. 'Did you intend to?' she queried, offering deliberate temptation as she lifted her arms and linked them carefully at his nape, only to gasp as his mouth closed over hers with deep, drugging possession.

He gave no quarter, and she expected none as she met and matched his ardour, exulting in the feel and taste of him, the heavy thudding beat of his heart as it pounded against her own in unison, the sheer sensation of knowing he was hers. It was a heady power, one she knew she would never choose to abuse.

Minutes later she cried out as his mouth left hers to trail down her throat, and she arched her neck to allow him access to the sensitive hollows, gasping as he teasingly nipped delicate skin, then slid to begin an open-mouthed suckling at one silk-covered breast that caught her slender frame in a paroxysm of sensation.

'You are wearing too many clothes, *mi mujer*,' he chastised huskily minutes later as his fingers began to deal with the buttons on her blouse.

'Hmm,' she agreed with a delicious smile. 'So are you.' Her eyes danced with wicked amusement. 'There's a problem,' she announced with seeming regret, and felt his fingers still as he looked at her in silent enquiry.

'Ana is serving dinner at seven.'

His eyes darkened with ill-concealed humour. 'Next,' he murmured huskily, 'you'll tell me you're hungry.'

She wrinkled her nose at him. 'We could eat first, then retire early.'

'Flattering, to be relegated second to food.'

'I promise I'll make it up to you,' Elise declared, and he smiled, the creases deepening as they slashed each cheek.

'Interesting.'

'It will be,' she teased. 'It's the reason I need to keep up my strength.'

His fingers moved to refasten slowly the buttons on her blouse, then he kissed her with such incredible gentleness that it was all she could do not to wind her arms up around his neck and tell him to make love to her *now*.

'Then let us go downstairs and sample what Ana has chosen to serve us.'

They ate a leisurely meal, deliberately pacing themselves, each increasingly aware of the moment they would rise from the table and go upstairs to their suite.

There was a sense of anticipation that became more acute with every passing minute, a sensual teasing as they indulged in a playful game.

More than once Alejandro paused in the process of eating to lift his glass and utter a salute in a drawled collection of Spanish words that required no interpreter to define them.

'After your son is born, you'll have to censor your words,' she chided with an attempt at severity, and failed miserably beneath the liquid warmth of his gaze.

'I have no intention of withholding from him how much I adore his beloved *mamá*.'

She had a mental image of a small dark-haired boy with mischievous dark eyes, running, laughing, infinitely loved by his parents. And later, God willing, there would be a little girl for him to protect and adore.

Elise speared the last segment of fruit from her plate and lifted it to her mouth, biting the firm flesh of deliciously fresh melon with a delicacy that brought a brilliant flaring to the eyes of the man seated opposite.

'I suppose you are going to insist I take coffee?'

Her eyes openly teased his, sparkling with unguarded humour. 'Caffeine,' she explained knowledgeably, 'is supposed to stimulate the brain.'

His dark gaze became languid, a displayed deception that didn't fool her in the slightest as he queried in a silky drawl, 'And it is my *brain* you particularly want to stimulate?'

She swallowed the last of the melon, then ran the edge of her tongue lightly over the curve of her lips. 'I would be disappointed,' she declared with slight emphasis, 'if you proved less than . . . capable,' she finished delicately.

His eyes became faintly hooded, and the edge of his mouth assumed an upward curve. 'Witch,' he responded with deliberate lightness as he sat back in his chair and savoured his wine.

Aware of his propensity to conduct a leisurely lovemaking, extending her pleasure to a point where she became wholly, solely *his*, before tipping them both over the edge into a state of passionate oblivion, she wondered at the wisdom of baiting him.

At that moment Ana entered the room and began clearing the table, her movements sure, deft, and unobtrusive.

'That was a lovely meal,' Elise complimented gently, and was rewarded with a pleased smile.

'*Gracias*. Will you have coffee here, or in the lounge?'

Elise glanced towards Alejandro, who merely raised one eyebrow in silent mockery as he transferred the responsibility for a decision.

'Would you mind bringing it out on to the terrace? It's such a beautiful evening.'

'My wife is a romantic,' Alejandro drawled, sparing Elise a long, thoughtful glance that curled her toes.

'The evening sunset,' Ana agreed with a slight nod. 'Such lovely colours.'

'Indeed,' he acknowledged, and his beautifully chiselled mouth widened slightly as he got to his feet and crossed round to assist Elise from her chair.

Seconds later, as they moved out on to the terrace, his arm curved lightly round her waist, its warm strength a tangible entity that crept through her skin and seemed to liquefy her bones.

The swimming-pool looked intensely blue in the soft fading light, its surface reflecting a mirrored sheen that was duplicated on the waters in the inner harbour.

Elise's gaze wandered out towards the horizon where ocean met sky, breathing in deeply the clean sea-air as she savoured the slight breeze that teased her hair and faintly stirred the leaves on various trees.

Alejandro shifted slightly to stand behind her, his hands linking protectively over her thickening waist as he drew her back against him.

She felt his lips brush her hair, then slip down to settle in the hollow at the edge of her neck as he teased the delicate flesh. Soft tremors shook her slim frame, and she leaned into him, loving the hard muscularity of his solid frame as he enclosed her within the cage of his arms.

To rest against him like this was heaven, and she was aware of the promise of passion, the strength of his control as he simply held her, content to allow her to savour the magic of nature as the sun slowly disappeared beyond the horizon in a brilliant flaring of orange and gold tinged with purple, before the silvery sky slowly darkened to an inky velvet.

The chink of crockery in the background was an intrusive sound they both acknowledged, and together they turned and slowly wandered towards a wide, cushioned two-seater as Ana poured Alejandro's coffee, then filled a glass with water from an iced pitcher for Elise.

'Goodnight, *señor, señora*.'

Alejandro sent Ana a warm smile. '*Gracias. Buenas noches*.'

When the housekeeper had returned indoors he leaned forward and spooned sugar into the dark aromatic brew, stirred, then cradled the cup in his hands.

Elise was strangely pensive. They had cleared up so many misconceptions but——

'There is something on your mind?'

It was a light, teasing query, and, suddenly brave, she took courage in both hands. 'Savannah.'

'What is it you want to know?'

His voice was a wry drawl, and in the semi-darkness it was difficult to gauge his mood. 'You were her lover?'

'Yes.'

It hurt more than she cared to admit, even now.

'A long time ago,' he qualified.

'She implied——'

'Innuendo coupled with distorted fact is a dangerous combination,' Alejandro interposed drily.

She had to ask. 'Did you love her?'

He didn't hesitate. 'No. Nor did she love me.' His eyes pierced hers, dark and faintly brooding.

Elise stared out into the darkness, hardly aware of the tracery of dimmed lamps that sprang to life around the grounds, highlighting the gardens.

'She still wants you,' she opined slowly.

'Savannah dislikes conceding defeat.'

She recalled the cruelly spoken words, spiteful in their intention, deliberately chosen to destroy by a woman who was unlikely to find personal happiness with any one man.

Elise rose slowly to her feet. 'If you've finished your coffee, I'll return the tray to the kitchen.'

'I'll take it.' He moved with lithe ease, and once indoors he activated security before following her through to the rear of the house.

The kitchen gleamed from Ana's meticulous care, and it only took a few minutes for Elise to load their cups into the dishwasher and rinse out the coffee-pot.

She was conscious of Alejandro's studied gaze, and she tilted her chin to meet it, her eyes clear pools of liquid emerald ringed with gold.

There were words she wanted to say, achingly poignant and straight from the heart, yet they seemed locked in her throat. For a moment she hesitated, then she slowly extended her hand and caught hold of his, threading her fingers through his own. 'I want to make love with you.'

His fingers tightened, then he raised her hand to his lips, and Elise saw the blaze of emotion evident in the darkness of his gaze. Deep, heartfelt, and electrifyingly primitive.

Then he curved an arm beneath her knees and lifted her high against his chest.

A slow, burning excitement unfurled deep within and radiated through her body until she felt achingly alive. 'I can walk,' she protested with a soft laugh.

His smile was a thing of beauty, warm and passionate, his eyes almost black. 'Indulge me.'

Her lips were so close to his throat that it was an irresistible temptation to rest them against the warm pulsing cord and savour the deep thudding beat. Gently she circled it with her tongue, then drew it carefully into her mouth.

'Do you want to be ravished *here*?' Alejandro threatened huskily as he gained the stairs.

Elise gave a soft exultant laugh and bestowed a rain of soft kisses along the edge of his jaw. 'The bed might be more comfortable,' she teased, loving his strength, the sheer force of his raw masculinity.

On reaching the main suite he let her slip gently to her feet and drew her close within the circle of his arms.

His mouth closed over hers with infinite gentleness, then hardened as she melted against him, taking possession of her mouth in a manner that left her in no doubt of his feelings.

At last he lifted his head, and she could only look at him in mesmerised wonder as his fingers worked the buttons on her blouse, then dealt with the clasp fastening the contoured strip of silk and lace supporting her breasts.

They felt heavy, each dusky peak swollen as it ached, hungering for his touch.

'You're beautiful.' He traced the curve, shaping it with a reverence that brought the prick of tears, and she blinked rapidly to dispel the threatened spill.

Slowly she lifted a hand and trailed her fingers along the strong thrust of his jaw, tracing the firm chin, the faint indentation, then the chiselled shape of his mouth.

Nothing—no one—mattered. Not Savannah, nor any of the other women who had inevitably shared part of his life.

Who was it who had said you had to make each day count?

The quote and its source eluded her. The message, however, did not.

Her eyes searched his, seeing the watchful stillness in those dark eyes, the hint of pain. 'I tried very hard not to love you,' she declared in a voice that was unbearably husky. She swallowed the sudden lump that rose in her throat. 'I don't remember when it changed, only that it did,' she continued, without any pretence at hiding her emotions. 'Now I know I can't live without you.'

Alejandro reached for her, his hands shaking slightly as they slid to frame her face. 'I want to love you, be with you, for as long as it takes to reach forever. *Dios mediante*,' he vowed huskily.

'Yes,' she agreed simply, her heart in her eyes as she brought his head down to meet hers, and there was the hint of an impish smile softening the curve of her mouth as it parted to receive his. 'Are we through talking?'

'Definitely,' he murmured as his mouth closed over hers, his actions proving more than mere words could ever convey...

BRIDE'S BAY RESORT

UNLOCK THE DOOR TO GREAT ROMANCE AT BRIDE'S BAY RESORT

Join Harlequin's new across-the-lines series, set in an exclusive hotel on an island off the coast of South Carolina.

Seven of your favorite authors will bring you exciting stories about fascinating heroes and heroines discovering love at Bride's Bay Resort.

Look for these fabulous stories coming to a store near you beginning in January 1996.

Harlequin American Romance #613 in January
Matchmaking Baby by Cathy Gillen Thacker

Harlequin Presents #1794 in February
Indiscretions by Robyn Donald

Harlequin Intrigue #362 in March
Love and Lies by Dawn Stewardson

Harlequin Romance #3404 in April
Make Believe Engagement by Day Leclaire

Harlequin Temptation #588 in May
Stranger in the Night by Roseanne Williams

Harlequin Superromance #695 in June
Married to a Stranger by Connie Bennett

Harlequin Historicals #324 in July
Dulcie's Gift by Ruth Langan

Visit Bride's Bay Resort each month wherever Harlequin books are sold.

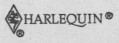

HARLEQUIN®

HARLEQUIN PRESENTS®

It's the wedding of the month!

The latest in our tantalizing new selection of stories...

Wedlocked!

Bonded in matrimony, torn by desire...

Watch for:

#1817 SECOND-BEST BRIDE
by Sara Wood

Did she *dare* take this man?

Available in June wherever Harlequin books are sold.

HARLEQUIN PRESENTS®

Ever felt the excitement of forbidden fruit?
Ever been thrilled by feverish desire?

Then you'll enjoy our selection of
dangerously sensual stories.

Take a chance on

Dangerous Liaisons

Falling in love is a risky affair!

Watch for:

#1818 FLIRTING WITH DANGER
by Kate Walker

Who was the good guy, who was her secret admirer...
were they one and the same man?

Available in June wherever Harlequin books are sold.

DL-F